ONE MAN'S JOURNEY

THE EXPERIENCES OF
AN AFRICAN AMERICAN
NEW YORK STATE
PAROLE OFFICER

ANTHONY JOHNSON

iUniverse

ONE MAN'S JOURNEY
THE EXPERIENCES OF AN AFRICAN AMERICAN
NEW YORK STATE PAROLE OFFICER

iUniverse books may be ordered through booksellers or by contacting:

iUniverse
1663 Liberty Drive
Bloomington, IN 47403
www.iuniverse.com
1-800-Authors (1-800-288-4677)

ISBN: 978-1-4917-9215-5 (sc)
ISBN: 978-1-4917-9216-2 (e)

Library of Congress Control Number: 2016904771

Print information available on the last page.

iUniverse rev. date: 08/15/2016

CONTENTS

FOREWORD

I thought about writing a book where the Parole Officers were not only portrayed as heroes but were also able to show the skills he/she possessed, for some time, even while still working as one. Movies and Television seem to always portray Parole Officers as overworked.underpaid, incompetent civil servants, who are passing the time until they can receive their pensions and can get out. This could not be further from the truth. Parole and Probation organizations are important parts of the Criminal Justice System.

I found that being a New York State Parole Officer was interesting, challenging and at times adventurous. Parole Officers wear many different hats in the performance of their jobs. They have to be social workers, peace officers, investigators, prosecutors, addiction specialists, litigators, psychologists, and mentors. How many jobs require someone to be knowledgeable in so many different professions? Yet the general public knows little of what we do. The information gathered and stored by Parole Officers has been vital to the apprehension and conviction of many criminals who have committed heinous crimes.

It is my hope that although this is a fictional account of events. the reader of the book will get a different slant on what Parole Officers encounter daily and let them know that most officers are educated, dedicated, competent, organized, and skilled at their chosen profession.

This book is dedicated to all Parole and Probation Officer wherever they reside in this country.

CHAPTER 1

"END ZONE'S BACKGROUND"

This is a story about the life of Terrance "End Zone" Jackson a moderately intelligent man born into a hard working God loving family. His grandparents both maternal and paternal were members of the same Baptist church. His parents met in that church. His paternal grandfather Fred Jackson made a decent living as the chauffeur and gentlemen's man for a wealthy and prominent family in Philadelphia. He was born in Waynesboro Georgia where he was heralded as a great baseball player in the old Negro league. Had the all white national baseball league been recruiting Negro players he probably would have made it to the major league. His maternal grandfather Malachi Patterson also made a good living as a construction worker who contributed to the building of some of the most famous buildings and bridges built in Philadelphia, New Jersey and New York during the 1950's and 60's. These men knew and understood the value of family and imparted these values to their children.

Terrance spent most of his childhood and adolescence trying to fit in. He knew he was neither the nicest looking kid in the neighborhood, nor the smartest kid, but on the other hand he didn't feel ugly or dumb. He spent most of his time playing basketball, touch football, baseball, and even half ball. Half ball was a popular game in his neighborhood in Philly because it only took two people to play, a pitcher and a batter. Half ball was a game where you took a rubber ball cut it in half and pitched the halves to the batter who used a broom stick handle as a bat. If the half ball got past the pitcher on the fly without it being caught there were designated areas for a first, second, third base and home runs. Terrance dreamed of becoming a pro football player some day because he felt that was his best sport because of his quickness. Never mind that at 12 he probably weighed less than 100 pounds. He thought he would grow by high school to be heavy enough to compete along with his speed. He also figured out early that the girls were attracted to athletes, so he spent as much time as he could at the various playgrounds, playing sports. Although Terrance's parents believed the way to success was through education, he found studying and school boring. If not for his parents he probably would have been a drop out which many times because of the lack of an education and opportunity could lead to criminal behavior. Since he was mentally lazy he thought the best way to make his family proud was to excel at sports. Terrance's mother and maternal grandfather had a flair for dress so he picked up that trait early. Nice clothes made him feel good about himself and since he was fortunate enough to have two working parents that could afford to buy him clothes three times a year, Easter for church, in the fall for school, and Xmas. He also saw the attention that he got from girls when he was wearing nice things. On weekends when he spent time at his grandparent's homes he would watch both his grandfathers meticulously evaluate what suit they would wear to church on Sunday. What tie went best with the suit? What shoes to wear? This was the only time that these hard working men had the opportunity of free expression during the week. Since his paternal grandfather was employed as a gentlemen's man he taught Terrance how to coordinate his shoes, tie and handkerchief with his suit. Since Terrance's father was always working one of his uncles taught him how to tie his tie. All of these skills would become useful later in his life.

Church was a place of refuge and solace for both sides of Terrance's family. All of his grandparents belonged to the same church. Both of his grandfathers were on the deacon board and his parents met in that church. Sundays were a family day starting with the services, long services. To a 7 or 8 year old 4 hours in church seemed like a lifetime. Terrance later in life attributed this to his dislike for religious services. Those memories of long services that he didn't understand or couldn't relate to were always with him. He remembered the time he had his head laying in his grandmother's lap half asleep during a service when she leaped to her feet and jumped in the aisle and starting shaking and screaming "yes lord !yes lord!". The church members called it receiving the Holy Ghost but to a young child who had never seen his grandmother act like this before, it was traumatic. It was never truly explained to him why grandmom acted like she did that one time in church. These types of unexplained situations helped reinforce the things that he questioned about religion. Terrance was never hooked on religion but participation was expected by his family. Once he was of an age to make his own decision about whether or not he wanted to go he decided to stop as he saw so much hypocrisy with the members including some of the people in his family. They were holy every Sunday and sinning like hell during the week. He felt that anyone could make a few mistakes, people are human, but if you commit the same sins over and over again at what point is there a penalty for your behavior. What would be God's penalty? The more he read about history the more he questioned how God could have allowed the savage enslavement of black people, how could he have allowed the extermination of the American Indian; weren't wars fought over religion? If so why since most religions preached peace. These, among many other questions he felt were unanswered? It was because of these questions it made him rethink the whole concept of religion because to him it made no rational sense. Is God good when he allows babies to be beaten or starved to death, he thought. Is God good when he allows decent people to be robbed or killed by bad people for a watch, coat, or a pair of sneakers? Why would an all powerful God allow a woman to be beaten and raped? He felt fortunate to have been a part of a loving caring family but everyone did not experience these blessings-why? Does God have his chosen ones and is everyone else left to survive the best way they know how? Why are some people blessed with intelligence and others left in ignorance? Does God have control over these circumstances and incidents? He wondered how believing in someone that you never met, nor even heard speak empowered you to take care of yourself? Should not the here and now be more important than the here after? Since he grew up watching strong women such as his mother, grandmothers, and aunts, and it was said that God made man in his image, why did he have to be a man? These questions were constantly on his mind and unanswered to his satisfaction. He thought about the black homes that he visited as a child where he saw pictures on the wall of a white man with long dirty brown hair and was told that this was the image of Jesus. If a person of color grows up believing that this is the image of God, does that subliminally contribute to any feelings they might have of inferiority, he questioned? He was glad that his parents, although believing in God themselves, never posted any pictures such as that in their home. His father once told him that men who use reason to understand religion would never understand it. His father was also one of those men who even though he went to church and said his prayers had his own doubts about the concept. Going to church can't hurt as long as you come away from the service with something good, he told his son. Terrance thought his father was smart to think the way he did because it was a way of covering all the bases. Terrance felt that if he lived the type of life written about in the bible and other religious books, even though he didn't believe, God would understand. After all wasn't that the basis of most of the commandments? In spite of all these questions he had a profound respect for religion. He saw how his parents and grandparents drew strength from their belief in God. He saw that true believers used religion as a way of explaining the unexplainable. He could accept that in others but for him he reasoned that most tragedies happened because of human behavior. Then there were accidents that happen that are nobody's fault.

Tragically losing a few childhood friends at early ages made him question why God would let bad things happen to good people. "Its Gods will" was not acceptable to him. The church was the center of his family's universe. He was thankful that these same people, when he got older respected his feelings. There were times he enjoyed spending hours at family dinners debating and trying understanding religious belief. Like most families Terrance's family had its share of alcoholics, thieves, drug addicts, hustlers and philanderers. As Terrance got older he tried to understand and felt empathy for some of his wayward relatives that no one wanted to be around. His mother had always shown that same empathy when others in the family did not. She practiced what she believed. Terrence tried to balance what he saw his mother practice with what he learned in the street. You care but you don't let yourself be used.

Terrence's childhood was relatively without conflict. Although he was given a lot of freedom as a teenager by his parents, he rarely got into any serious trouble. In later years he wondered had he been smart or just been lucky because he hung out with a bunch of crazy guys. For instance there was the time when he was twenty years old and home from college for the summer break when one of his childhood friends named Paul came by his house and invited him to come and hang out with him. Paul was a nice guy most of the time, but he had a tendency to exaggerate when telling stories. His story telling was entertaining but sometimes got him into a great deal of trouble. His constant diatribes full of lies were told so often that his friends nicknamed him "Paul Bunyan" after the storybook character known for telling tall tales. He once told Terrance that while he was in Vietnam during his time in the service he saw a dinosaur eating potato salad through a barbed wire fence. Terrance laughed so hard when told this story that he fell out of the chair he was sitting in. He knew Paul was lying but the story was funny. It was later explained to Terrance that in Vietnam there were giant lizards who were vegetarians. These lizards many times would eat the vegetables grown by farmers, in the region, through the fences that were put there to keep them out. In Paul's mind after smoking enough reefers they were dinosaurs.

Paul convinced Terrance to hang out by telling him that he had a couple of bottles of wine and some beer in his car that they could drink. The thought of free booze, when you are a broke ass college student, had always been attractive to Terrance, so he went along for the ride and drink. During their travels they ran into two other friends who Terrance had not seen since coming home for the summer. The two men decided to join them. After drinking and laughing, while crusing around their neighborhood, they decided that they all wanted to play some pinochle. Since they all lived at home with their parents, they knew what they wanted to do in any of those homes was not permissible, so they decided to go to the only place where they could do what they wanted, smoke reefer, drink till drunk, and curse. This was the apartment of the "Vach man." Vach was several years older than most of them, but he liked hanging out with a younger crew. Paul called Vach from a pay phone to find out if he was at home. He was home and told the guys to come on over. After drinking a bit more and smoking a few joints in Vach's apartment the card playing began. An hour or so after they were playing cards there was a knock at the door.

When the door was answered it was another friend of the crew they called "Donnie doll." As everyone else in the crew who had a nickname or street name Donnie got his because he was a light skin black man with wavy hair which the ladies seemed to have been attracted to ever since they were all kids. The crew all said that he looked like a doll, thus the name. Another thing that Donnie was known for was screwing every woman that he could. "I don't turn nothing down but my collar, short, tall, blind, crippled or crazy I'll take it if they want to give it," was his favorite saying. Donnie wasn't alone when he entered Vach's apartment. He had a young woman with him. She was 5 feet 5 inches tall, 125 lbs., and built. He didn't introduce her to any of the fellows, but asked Vach could he use his bedroom? Vach said yes and pointed him towards the room. By now Terrance had lost a few card games, and since he started getting high before all of his comrades he was starting to come down, so he decided to go into the living room and lay down on the sofa for a little nap. He had been asleep for about and hour and a half when he was awakened by one of his boys who told him it was his turn. Half groggy he thought he meant his turn back on the card table, but after clearing his eyes he saw that his friend was standing over him sweating heavily while trying to put his pants back on. It didn't take Terrance long to figure out what was happening. The apartment smelled of sex, and there were signs that Donnie wasn't the only person in the apartment who had gotten his rocks off. Just to be clear Terrance asked "What is going on?" He was told that Donnie left the apartment after he got what he wanted telling his boys as he walked out of the door that they could all get some if they wanted because the young lady was still sleep in bed. When you get a bunch of high horny young men together with an offer like that it can be a recipe for trouble. Everyone else in the apartment had a taste and it was now Terrance's turn. Terrance first sarcastically thought how considerate it was of his friends to leave him sloppy lasts. He then came to his senses and declined the offer, after which he went back to sleep. He was never into pulling trains on women or group sex, at least within his limited experience; so the offer didn't appeal to him. The next time his friends woke him up they told him it was time to go. As he was getting himself together he overheard the discussion concerning who was going to take the young woman home because she had no money and no ride. Paul decided that he had no choice but to transport her since he and Vach were the only people in the apartment with wheels and Vach was already at home. To Terrance's surprise when the woman came out of the bedroom she was crying and appeared to be disheveled. He also observed as he followed her out of the apartment that the white pants she was wearing were split up the back on the seam so she had to hold them together with her hand as she walked. He was not the only person in the crew who made these observations, so as everyone approached the building elevator they began jockeying to position themselves in the back as they rode down to the ground floor. They didn't want the woman to now get a good look at them in the elevator light. Terrance grinned because he now knew what was going on, and he also knew that he had not been a part of whatever went on in Vach's bedroom. When the elevator opened his friends literally ran to Paul's car in the evening darkness. No one wanted to sit in the front seat of the car as they figured that the young lady that they had just finished ravishing would be sitting there. Terrance watched these three men sprint across the parking lot like they were in the Penn Relays. He laughed again because he knew they were scared as hell. They now appeared to be worried about the consequences of their actions. Paul's car had bucket seats in the front and since there were 5 people riding plus the driver one person had to sit on the console. It ended up that the young woman shared the front seat with Terrance and Paul. As they rode towards their first destination Terrance noticed how quiet everyone was in the car. The only sound was the Motown music playing on the car radio. He then decided to stir things up a bit by messing with his friends. He knew that if the situation was reversed they would do the same to him. He started off by asking the woman her name and was she alright? She told him in a soft voice that her name was June and that she was "O K". Terrance was empathetically concerned about her partly, because he had two sisters of his own, and he wouldn't want this to happen to them. It was now time to mess with his boys. He asked her next speaking in a loud voice so the fellows in the back seat could hear. "Why did you mess around with Donnie Doll? Didn't you know his reputation? If I had been you I would only date him if I had my own wheels so he couldn't leave me somewhere stranded." The more Terrance talked to June the more he could see out of the corner of his eye his friends sliding down in the back seat. Paul while driving with his left hand, kept his right hand up shading his face. Although Terrance did not want to make light of the situation it took every bit of control that he had not to laugh out loud at his friends, every time he turned and looked at them in the back of the car. They finally arrived at June's house and Terrance slid over to let her out of the car. As she walked up the front steps to her house she began to cry again. One of the guys in the back seat all of a sudden developed a conscience and blurted out "Shouldn't we wait to make sure she gets into her house safely before we pull off?" Hearing this Terrance couldn't hold it any longer breaking out in loud laughter. He then turned to them and said "Yawl in trouble!" For the rest of the ride to take each man home they tried to convince each other that they did nothing wrong. Terrance was the last to be dropped off.

The next day Terrance was sitting on his front porch when Paul pulled up in his car and runs up to join him. He immediately opened the conversation with the question "Did you hear what happened to us last night after I dropped you off?" Terrance responded no and then Paul told him, "Man I was sleep when my father woke me up and told me that the police were down stairs and wanted to speak to me." When he walked downstairs to the front door June was standing there with four cops. When she pointed him out he was placed on a wall, searched, and then handcuffed. From there he was led to a police van. When he got inside the van he saw Donnie already seated in cuffs. They subsequently rode around the neighborhood and picked up everyone who had been in Vach's apartment. Everyone except Terrance. As Paul described what happened Terrance thought how lucky he was to not at least been called in for questioning, even though he didn't witness anything. Sleeping off a high had definitely been an advantage. Paul further explained that they were all saved because it just so happened, that Donnie's father was a police officer. Once his father got involved his fellow officers made June out to be slut who wanted to have sex with multiple partners. As a result of the men being set free June's two brothers ended up getting arrested after they made a scene in the police station because they were upset nothing was done about their sister's rape. Oh yeah, the police kept Vach on some unrelated charges.

On one occasion when Terrance was in his early twenties his empathetic feelings were lost to the reality of the street. He had a cousin a few years younger than him who spent every dime he had on crack cocaine. His mother nicknamed him Bubba after his father who was never around. On this particular occasion Bubba's mother had enough of his trifling behavior and she kicked him out of her house. Although Terrance and Bubba did not travel in the same circle he decided to let his cousin stay with him on a temporary basis. That arrangement didn't last long when Terrance came home one day only to find that his brand new Sony television was gone. He knew right away who took it, so Terrance called the one friend he knew could help him get back his television. Bucky Grant was well known in the community for being a gentle giant at 6'6 and 250 lbs., all muscle. He and Terrance played on the same high school football team, and after high school they remained good friends. Bucky was also known to be a person that you didn't want to get angry. He was a member of the Black Panther Party and also carried a gun everywhere that he went. On a leather strapped necklace around his neck he had a 50 caliber machine gun bullet. Terrance knew Bucky was the man for this job. On an occasion when they were hanging out in a bar one night there was a confrontation between one of their crew and another guy in the bar. The argument spilled out into the street where everyone was verbally threatening everyone. Everybody was talking shit except Bucky who stood quietly, just watching the commotion until the guy who started the trouble looked his way and said "Don't think that I won't fuck up big boy too!" Bucky said not a word but walked up to him and shot him point blank in the chest. The big mouth hit the ground from the shot, bounced up and ran up the street and around the corner leaving one of his shoes in the process. Naturally after the shot everyone scattered. The next day, and for few weeks after that incident Terrance looked through the newspapers for any signs of the shooting. There never was any. Once again Terrance figuratively and literally dodged a bullet.

Terrance called Bucky and explained the situation with his TV and told him he had an idea of where he could find his cousin. Bucky told him to come and pick him up and he would watch his back. The two rode around surveilling the local crack areas. Eventually they spotted Bubba standing on a corner. They pulled up in front of him and as they both got out of the car Bucky told Terrance to open the trunk, which he did. Terrance then approached his cousin and began to question him about his missing TV. When Bubba denied knowing anything about the set Bucky immediately picked him up flipped him on his shoulder and threw him in the trunk of the car head first. He closed the trunk then turned to Terrance and said "Let's go!" All of the crack heads and dealers who were standing on the corner, when Terrance and Bucky pulled up just looked. Some of them may have been high but they all knew better than to mess with Bucky. Terrance drove to a secluded area where they pulled Bubba out of the trunk. He had no intentions of really inflicting serious injuries to his cousin although he was mad as hell. He also had no idea as to what Bucky had in mind, although he knew what he was capable of doing. When Bubba continued to deny any knowledge of the missing TV Bucky pushed up the threat level a notch. He made Bubba kneel on the ground after which he placed his pistol to the back of his head. He then said to Bubba "I am tired of your ass lying about the TV" as he cocked the hammer. Before Terrance could stop him from killing his cousin over a television Bubba yelled out "Don't kill me, I'll tell you where the TV is!" Bucky made Bubba climb back into the trunk of the car for the ride to the place where the television was sold. After some negotiations Terrance ended up paying 50 dollars to the man who had the TV in order to get it back. Needless to say when Bubba came back to Terrance's apartment he found his clothes on the steps and the locks changed. On the ride home after getting the TV back, Bucky told Terrance he wasn't going to kill his cousin but he knew that very few men could stand up to the stress of having a gun pressed against the back of their heads . He then said "So now let's go smoke some reefer and drink some liquor while we watch your TV."

Terrance got his nickname "End zone" when he played football at Germantown High School in Philadelphia. He did achieve his dream of playing football with a very talented team with a good coach. He ran back kickoffs and punt returns and broke a record in his senior year for the most run backs for touch downs, consequently getting the name from his teammates of

"End Zone" because they said he spent a lot of time there. He still wasn't a big guy but he made up for it with his speed. Terrance spent his high school years concentrating on football, although he was interested in girls who were all over him because he was an athlete, he was more interested in moving his football career to the next level. He wasn't a eunuch. He did get his cherry busted while in high school, but women just were not his focus. He also thought years later that his focus on sports probably saved him from doing too much drinking and smoking at an early age. He was sure that some of his friends took years off of their lives because they did too many unhealthy things too early.

When it was time for college Terrance continued to think of school as a pathway to professional football. It didn't matter that he wasn't that tall or that he wasn't that heavy. He felt he could outrun those big guys like he did in high school. He wasn't recruited by any college teams but he was invited by the coach of Florida A. & M. University to try out for the team. Terrance spent the majority of his life in the North East part of the country in a neighborhood where he wasn't exposed to racial prejudice except from the cops. His high school was 35 per cent Jewish, 40 percent African American and the rest made up of people of other various ethnic backgrounds. Most of the kids got along well. Terrance didn't venture out of his neighborhood that often but he felt that he could go just about anywhere he wanted. The operative words were "just about anywhere". While in high school Terrance met this beautiful young black girl at a party, named Sheila. She had moca colored skin and a face and body that was unbelievable for a 16 year old girl. He was surprised when he found out she was attracted to him. He fell in love with her as soon as she spoke to him. She was perfect, but there was a problem. She lived in West Philadelphia which was on the opposite side of Philadelphia and not very friendly towards the people from his neighborhood. Sheila was visiting her cousin when she and her two sisters, who also were also fine, were invited to the party. To make things worse during the football season Terrance scored the winning touch down between Germantown and West Philly High Schools, so he was a marked man in that neighborhood. Terrance was not going to let those obstacles interrupt his love life. The first time he went to visit Sheila he had to take two buses and the train. He didn't have any problems walking through her neighborhood on the way to her house as he thought to himself "Hell this ain't that bad," on with romance. He met Sheila's mother, and stayed for dinner. When it was time to leave he was standing by the front door getting a kiss and copping a feel when out of the corner of his eye he saw 5 guys standing in front of the house. They didn't appear to be a reception committee, at least not a positive one. Terrance told Sheila to just stand in the door 'til he walked away. She initially didn't know why until she saw the boys, all of whom she knew, standing on the side walk in front of her home. Terrance walked down the steps already in his red zone as he was looking around and developing his tactics to avoid and escape getting hurt. Sheila yelled out to the boys on the ground"Please leave him alone, he's my friend!" Terrance was not sure if the plea had any impact when one of the guys said to him. "We're not going to fuck with you this time,'cause we like the way you play ball, but don't come around here again." With that they let him go. As Terrance walked back to the train he was already thinking about how he was going to see Sheila again in spite of what just happened. Months passed and Terrance and Sheila saw each other on a regular basis. Terrance avoided getting his ass kicked by never going to see her unless he could borrow a car from a family member or a friend. He didn't know any gang that could out run a car, plus the car gave him a rolling bedroom. Sometimes Sheila met him at neutral spots. Eventually there was an occasion when Terrance couldn't borrow a car but wanted to see her. He decided to take a chance and ride public transportation. Once again with out any problems he made it to her house. However when he got ready to leave, who was standing outside the house? Four of the same five guys who had given him the warning. Terrance knew that he had to leave her house because it was late —too late to try and call the cavalry from his neighborhood. Most of them were probably high now and doing just what he came to Sheila's to do. He examined the guys on the ground closely and then told Sheila to ask her mother to come to the door so that he could say goodbye. She followed his instructions but it didn't work as her mother yelled good bye from her bedroom in the back of the house. When Terrance pretended not to hear her she eventually came out of the bedroom in her robe and said in an annoyed voice "GOOD NIGHT TERRANCE!!" This was Terrance's opening as he backed down the steps waving good bye. He figured that the boys on the ground would be hesitant about beating him up in front of Sheila's mom as she was well respected in her neighborhood. When he got to the side walk he took off running like he was on the football field. The four guys took off after him while he heard someone yell "Get that mother fucker!" By the time Terrance got to the train he had lost his pursuers. He had previously observed that these guys didn't look to be athletic so if he could get a running start, he could out run them to the train. His assessment was right. As he rode away on the train and looked out of the window, he felt a sigh of relief, and at the same time he laughed at how slow those guys were.

CHAPTER 2

"A WHOLE DIFFERENT WORLD"

Terrance decided to make the trip to Tallahasse, Florida and try out for the fooball team. His parents were happy to finance the trip even though they knew that his reason for going had nothing to do with getting an education. They reasoned if you get the body there the head would come around. Terrance had to change planes in Atlanta, Georgia on his ride to Florida. The first thing he saw as he got off the plane was a billboard. On the billboard was a knight in white armor riding a white horse with a white hood covering his face and head. The caption over the rider read "Welcome to Klan Country". Terrance had watched the civil rights movement on TV. He also saw Dr. Martin Luther King be interviewed on television a few times. It was the 1960's. His parents even belonged to the NAACP, but he had never experienced racism so up close and personal. He froze for a second in the plane door after seeing the billboard and wondered if he made the right decision coming to the south.

He then thought hell I've come this far, might as well go all the way.

Terrance arrived on the campus and was shown around by one of the assistant coaches. He had never been to Florida before and he thought the campus and the surrounding areas were the most beautiful he had ever seen. The women on campus were all tanned and built like they stepped out of model magazines. This was even more of a motivating factor to make the team and stay at this college. Terrance worked hard during the football practices. He had never seen so many 200 lbs. plus guys who were so fast. He also encountered prejudice on the football field for the first time when he realized that many of the players on the team who were from the south resented the ball players from northern cities like New Jersey, Philly, and New York. Because of their feeling about their team mates from north of the Mason Dixon line they collaborated in their efforts to stop them from making the team. For this reason the football practices were brutal. This was a time in football before the leagues were cognizant of protecting players from anymore harm than necessary. Dirty tactics were condoned, in fact they were expected. What you did on the field to defeat the opponent was accepted as long as you didn't get caught. To a guy weighing 170 lbs playing against guys 200 to 300 lbs. plus, who didn't like you just because of where you were born, it was intimidating. This was not only brutal but dangerous. Terrance never knew of any incidents where a player was killed but he did know of players receiving permanent disabilities from playing the game. Besides what was done to him, he witnessed other players from northern cities get hit with illegal low blows. He saw players from the north get their hands or feet stepped on at the end of plays,or a southern player not block for a runner from the north, so that they could get creamed by another player on the opposing side, and many other actions that could potentially end a players career. In spite of these circumstances he was still determined to make the team. He was informed and warned about what was going on by a teammate who was from Tampa, Florida who he had befriended. He explained to Terrance that the players and students from the North, had histories, because of the experiences in Northern big cities that made them more sophisticated. This sophistication made them attractive to southern women, as well as their understanding of the politics of campus living. After all, most of the players on the team were simple cock strong country boys. One night over a bottle of wine one of his team mates from Valdosta, Georgia told him that he had never seen snow accept on television. Terrance was shocked to hear this story as he grew up living in an area where he saw snow every winter, and he took it for granted that everyone had simular experiences. His Christmas holiday memories were filled with thoughts of snow ball fights, scarfs, hats, gloves, rubber boots and winter coats.

Since football was such a competitive and hands on sport it was easy for the players to focus their anger and rage on others. Many of the players were not interested in getting an education. They were there to play football and make the NFL. Terrance understood because when he arrived at the school that was his intention too. He later observed that in the off season many of the players seemed lost. A week before school was to start the final cuts were made to the football team. Terrance lasted to the last cut and was confident that he had made the team. He walked into the gym where the final cuts were announced on a bulletin board. He looked at the board and couldn't believe it when his name was among those let go from the team. He stood there in shock reading the names on the list of those who made the team several times hoping that he missed seeing his name. It wasn't there! Terrance now thought that he should go and talk to the defensive coach who had given him high marks for most of what he did and he was sure that the coach had some say so in who made the team. He knocked on the coach's door and was told to enter. The coach didn't seem surprised as he said "Ah Terrance you are one of the people after reading the list of who made the last cut that I expected to hear from ." He told Terrance to have a seat. "Listen son I liked your attitude about playing football from the day I met you. However that is not enough on this level. Yes you are fast, but there are others on the team faster. Yes you know how to defend against offensive ends, but there are players on the team that do it better and they are bigger than you. I thought long and hard about my decision to let you go, but my priority is the team." He then asked Terrance did he have enough money to pay for his first semester? Terrance told him that he had been approved for a student loan as he remembered the argument he had with his mother over applying for the loans as he felt he wasn't going to need them because he was getting an athletic scholarship. His mother was a music teacher in the Philadelphia school system so she knew what had to be done if she wanted her son to succeed in spite of his self. Terrance walked out of the coach's office shocked that he had been cut from the team. How would he explain this to his family and friends when he told every body how sure he was that he would make the team. The fact that he had been extremely succussful with sports in Philly made this even more shocking. He walked to the local liquor store near campus and bought a couple bottles of Thunderbird, a popular cheap wine in Philly and then went looking for the local drug dealer. Finding drugs on most college campuses was never hard. He finally found the dealer and then bought a couple of five dollar bags of reefer, after which he went to his room where he proceeded to get blasted. He was glad that his roommate had gone out of town with his girlfriend so that he could have the room to himself. Hours passed and Terrance still had not come to grips with what happened to him. Although his body and mind were full of wine and reefer he had an epiphany. He thought back to what he said to himself when he saw the KKK billboard in Atlanta. "I've come this far, might as well go all the way". He further thought since he didn't know many people in Florida and they didn't know him, he could make himself into anyone that he wanted. No one on campus knew much about his background. He decided that he was going to use this to his advantage. This was also a way of avoiding going home and telling everyone that he failed. Hell, the weather was nice all year round, the women were beautiful, and the reefer was plentiful and cheap. What else could a nineteen year old black man want, he was thinking. He, however, wasn't thinking about his education.

Terrance had to move out of the dorm room that he had because it and the whole floor that he was on was reserved for the school athletes. He moved into another dormitory and into a room with a young man who would end up being his best friend through his college years. Billy Gent was from Jamaica, Queens in New York. He was 6,4 and as crazy as he was fun to be around. He had tried out the previous year for the basketball team and like Terrance was cut. They both shared their experiences with sports failure, and then Billy told Terrance that he thought his decision to stay in school was the right one. Besides the fact that the women and the campus were both pleasing to the eye, he felt there was a wealth of knowledge to be gained from the staff and the various students in the school. This was the first time anyone besides his parents mentioned anything related to getting an education. Even in high school none of his friends talked much about what they were going to do after high school. Many of them went to college, at least the ones that didn't go to jail. They just didn't talk about it. In many cases Terrance found out who was going to college or into the military only weeks before they left. Since Billy had been at FAMU (Florida A & M University) a year before Terrance he knew the ropes. He told Terrance who he thought was cool to be around and who to avoid. He also hung around with some of the professors, some of whom were only a few years older than most of the students. This was particularly strange to Terrance. He never dreamed he would be socializing with teachers. Hell some of them drank and smoked like he did. In the classroom however, these same teachers were brillant. One teacher in particular was so versed on history that she never brought a book to class except a roll book. When she completed her attendence she would say "Now where did we leave off during the last class", and proceed to lecture with amazing accuracy and in vivid detail. Naturally Terrance tried to take the classes of those he spent socializing with. He was looking for an easy way out. It ended working out that those classes were so interesting that he did well without receiving favor. Terrance decided that he would stay in school and change his image but the people he was exposed to early in his college days ended up being the ones that changed him. It wasn't that his childhood friends were not intelligent. They just never talked about intellectual issues. Sports, girls, and partying were the focus. Terrance did only just enough to get by in high school so that his parents wouldn't stop him from playing football. The crowd he was around now also chased women, talked about sports, got high, but they also talked about philosophy, politics, religion, math, science and jazz music. Terrance had been exposed to jazz music by some of his family. One of his uncles was a jazz pianist. He didn't like it, probably because it was not explained to him. Music without lyrics are left to ones interpretation. When it was explained to him by his fellow students he understood it and began to enjoy it. These same people forced Terrance to sometimes think outside of the box. Conformity was challenged. Terrance always thought that on the street people challenged conformity every day. It was a means of survival for them. The difference in his current setting was that these people wanted to challenge the existing power structure in ways that would make things better for all. Their idealism was infectious. These students and teachers came from many different types of backgrounds; wealthy homes, poor homes, homes with single parents, and homes like Terrance's with parents who had middle class values. During his time in school Terrance was once called by his father who asked him if he knew a guy by the name of Julius Neven? He told his father that he did and that Julius had changed his name to Abdul Muhummad. Terrance's father then explained to him that the FBI had come to the family home inquiring about him and their relationship. Some time later that same week Terrance told Abdul what his father told him. Adbul played dumb and told Terrance that he didn't know what that visit was all about. Some years later before they both graduated Abdul shared with Terrance that he came from an extremely poor family, and so in order to attend college he and two other guys robbed a bank in Boston. He used his share of the money to finance his college education. Abdul subsequently went on to medical school and became a doctor.

One of the most traumatic things that happened during Terrance's freshman year of college was the assassination of Dr. Martin Luther King Jr. Terrance was sitting in his dorm room preparing for finals when someone came running down the hallway yelling "they killed him, they killed him!" Terrance didn't know who he was talking about, but from the hallway he could hear over a radio in someone else's room that he was talking about Dr. King. Terrance's first reaction was confusion. He didn't know what he should do, so he walked back into his room trying to process what he just heard. It didn't take him long to make a decision, at least a temporary one. When he looked out of his dormitory room window he saw all the other dormitories emptying out, as students ran into the streets around the campus picking up sticks, bottles or anything that they could use as a weapon. Terrance basically followed the crowd out of curiousity. He had never been in nor witnessed a riot. He saw angry men go off the campus and just start pulling white people out of cars and beating them up. One old white man refused to open his car door and as he tried to drive away crashed into a pole. He still refused to exit his vehicle so the crowd turned the car over and pushed it into a ditch. When a few police cars arrived they were pelted with rocks and bottles. Terrance began to build up some anger of his own now as the reality of what happened set in, so he threw a couple of bottles at cops too. Another reality set in when someone starting firing shots at the cops. He remembered now that this was the south. Getting a gun was easy and legal. In Philly if you heard gun shots you ran in the other direction as quickly as possible. Terrance's instinct took over and he did just that, retreating back to the safety of campus. Running back he thought "I am not going to bring a rock to a gun fight." The Tallahassee Police Department regrouped within an hour and drove the rioting students back onto the campus. They did not attempt to enter the campus because it was state property which was out of their jurisdiction. They surrounded the campus with the help of other local police departments, staying just out of pistol and rifle range. Terrance was surprised to see so many students in possession of firearms. There were even students with bows and arrows. They shot arrows at the police from the trees on campus. By morning the word had gotten around that officials were closing down the school and sending everybody home. Any student who couldn't afford to go home was given a bus ticket to do so by the university. Terrance saw on tv that there were riots in many major cities all up the east coast of the United States including Washington DC. He and Billy stood in long lines on campus trying to call their homes to get money to travel. Hours later they got tired and decided to go off campus to a phone booth that they thought was in a safe area. There were three phone booths side by side so a couple of other guys also decided to go with them. They quickly walked down side streets avoiding any place that looked dangerous. Once they arrived at the booths Terrance, Billy and one of the other two guys entered the booths. Terrance called his father, and as they discussed what he was going to do, he happened to notice an old grey Ford station wagon slowly moving down the street in their direction. His instincts suggested that he should keep his eyes on the car even though he was talking on the phone. As the car came closer Terrance noticed that there were four white men riding in the car. When the car got to the corner where the phone booths were located a shot gun was pointed from the window. Fortunately the other three men with Terrance also saw the shotgun. Terrance didn't have time to exit the phone booth because it happened so fast, so his defensive position was to drop down low in the booth. From the shotgun came two consecutive blasts shattering the top of the booth that he was in. Terrance's father heard the shots through the phone and started yelling Terrance's name. Terrance quickly told his dad that he was alright and then told him to pay for a plane ticket which he could pick up at the Tallahasse airport. He then left the phone and along with his other friends ran back to campus. Fortunately none of them were injured. When Terrance got back to the campus he and Billy quickly started packing their bags while telling others in the dorm what happened. While Terrance was explaining what happened, one of the guys in his room said "Terrance look at your arm!" He then looked down and saw that his left shirt sleeve was bloody. He rolled up his sleeve and saw what appeared to be small holes in his arm. He wasn't aware of the injury while running back to the campus, and didn't feel any pain until he saw his arm. Abdul wrapped Terrance's arm in a towel and took him to the campus hospital. The doctor in the hospital removed four shot gun pellets from Terrance's arm. Terrance told the doctor to "Please hurry; I got a plane to catch." Terrance figured out that when he went down to cover himself in the phone booth the last part of his body to go down was his left arm, as he was holding the phone in that hand catching some shotgun pellets.

Although FAMU was predominantly a Black University there were some white folks going to the school. When Terrance got back to the dormitory to pick up his bags before leaving, he saw several National Guard soldiers on campus. They were there to escort the white students into the dorm to get their belongings, and then to escort them off of the campus safely. All of the soldiers were carrying M16 rifles and appeared to be ready to use them if necessary.

On the flight home the plane passed over Washington DC at a low altitude and Terrance saw what appeared to be fires burning in hundreds of locations. What he witnessed in the past 24 hours made him realize the magnitude of what had happened. He wondered how it would change the world in which he lived? He felt lucky to be alive after someone tried to take his life.

CHAPTER  3

"TIME TO FIGHT AGAINST RACISM"

The University was closed for a few weeks as result of the riots that took place. The school president called it "A cooling off period." It may have been that for him, but to the students and the people in the surrounding black communities and, black neighborhoods across America, things were not that cool. When Terrance returned to school he thought about some of the racist things that had happened to him since he arrived at the school in late August. He had originally blown them off as "shit that happens", but after the assassination of Martin Luther King Jr, he became more sensitive to acts of racism. He thought about how sheltered, naïve or both he had been while growing up. He was angry at himself for not taking the time to be more aware. He wished that he had been more in touch sooner with what had been going on nationally as it related to racism and prejudice. He thought back to his second day in Florida when he was walking to the Leon County Bank in down town Tallahassee when he noticed people running in his direction. What he didn't notice at first was that they were all black. Finally a young black man, who had been running stopped to warn him that the Klu Klux Klan was involved in a parade which was coming in his direction. He warned Terrance that if he was smart, he didn't want to be anywhere near those rednecks when they were parading. Terrance thanked him but did not immediately turn and run. He had seen Klan rallies on television, but never in person so he watched them march down the street in their white robes and hoods with someone in the lead carrying a holy cross on a staff. He turned and ran when he thought the parade was getting dangerously close.

On another occasion Billy and Terrance were hungry one night after smoking reefer and listening to music, so they decided to go off campus and get something to eat, as everything on the campus was closed except for the soda machines. There was gas station not to far off campus called the "Oil Well" where they had all types of vending machines. You could purchase chili dogs, hamburgers, hot dogs, and even hot soup. While they were facing the machines and deciding what to buy, several police cars pulled up as if they were chasing someone. Officers exited their vehicles and pointed shot guns and pistols at them while ordering them in a deep southern draw, not to move. Both of them had enough street smarts to know that the best thing to do was to follow their instructions. Anything less could result in serious injury to them, maybe even death. They knew those redneck cops were looking for an excuse to blow them away. The police approached them and slammed both of them against police cars while being searched. Since Terrance was now bent over the hood of a police car in handcuffs, he felt it was time to take a risk and ask the cops what it was that he was being accused of doing? A police officer responded, "You will find out later nigger", as he rachetted up the level of pain compliance by pulling up on the handcuffs attached to Terrance's wrists. They were placed in separate cop cars and driven to the local precinct, where they were placed in the same cell. They tried to understand why they just wanted to get something to eat, because they had the munchies, and were now sitting in jail cell at 2 o'clock in the morning. Billy eventually noticed that there were two brothers in the cell across from theirs. At the same time the police brought in two more black men and placed them in another cell. He figured that one of them must have given the cops some lip, because he was bleeding from the mouth and nose and had a knot on the side of his head. Billy asked the men in the cell across from his why were they arrested? They responded that they didn't know. They told Billy and Terrance that they were just walking down the street on their way home from work when the police pulled guns on them, handcuffed them without explanation, and brought them to the precinct. Terrance wanted to ask the cops permission to make a phone call. He had seen it happen on television so many times that he knew it was his right. Billy advised against it reminding him that he was in the south, in a place where the rules don't always apply. He didn't want to piss off the cops until he knew more about the situation. Terrance followed his lead but thought to himself "if this is what his grandparents had to accept while living down south it is no wonder they moved up north." He had unjustified altercations with Philly cops in the past but nothing on this level. A few hours later two white women were escorted through the cell block, by two police officers, stopping at each cell. The cell block was now full of black men. The women and the police escort made the rounds and then left the cell block without saying a word. Around 7 A.M. Terrance and Billy were awakened by a police officer who unlocked the cell and told them they were free to go. They were given back their property. They were not given any explanation for their arrest, or why they were detained over night; more importantly, to Terrance, no apology. He never really hated cops before because he avoided contact with them by being smart. His attitude now began to change. He was beginning to feel like the panthers felt "kill the pigs!" Over the next week Billy and Terrance talked with people, read the newspapers, and pieced together what happened. On the night in question a laundromat a mile or so from where they were arrested, was robbed by two armed black men who got away with a couple hundred dollars. The police arrested any two black men they encountered on the street who just happened to have been so unfortunate as to be together that night. The women they paraded through the cell block were the victims of the robbery, who were there to identify the stick up men. Billy and Terrance never found out if the crime was ever solved.

Terrance had another experience not too long after the encounter with Billy. One Sunday evening while sitting around in his dorm room with several other students, they began to talk about how they wished they had a television in one of their rooms that they could all watch. Vinny who was an electronic wizard, told the group that if he had the right materials he could build a television. He pointed out to the group that he could get many of the components, including a picture tube, legally, from the school. What he could not get was a shell to hold the picture tube. Someone in the group said that a local appliance store put old televisions out on the curb as trash to be collected on the weekends. He also suggested that there might even be parts that could be used in making the set. Everyone got worked up over this idea and decided since it was a slow night that four of them would get into a car and drive to the store to see if the information was true. Upon arriving at the store around 7PM, they saw several old televisions sitting on the curb in front of the store just as was suggested. The four men, including Terrance, got out of the vehicle and examined the old sets to see if any of them could be refurbished. They chose one and put it in the trunk of the car. Just as all four men went to get back into their car, two police cars pulled out of what seemed like nowhere, and blocked the car front and back. The police officers exited their cars, pulled the guns, and ordered the men to place their hands on tops of their heads . Although they were puzzled as to what they had done everyone complied. They all were aware of what could happen to black men who failed to comply with police instructions in the south. They were all searched and then placed in the police cars, two in one car and two in the second car. Terrance tried to explain to one of the officers who appeared to be approachable that his group was under the impression that the televisions were trash, but the officer didn't want to hear it. Terrance couldn't believe that this was happening to him again. He had been smart and lucky enough to avoid any contact with the criminal justice system for 19 years, and now within a few months time he was arrested twice. He now had second thoughts about attending school in the south. Did he make the right decision or should he take his black ass back to Philly, he thought. The four students were taken to Leon County Jail where they were booked and finger printed. They were informed that they were charged with Petit Larceny, the theft of property under a thousand dollars. They were all given orange jump suits to wear in exchange for their clothes and then placed in the same cell with two sets of bunk beds. They were further informed that they would go before a judge the next morning. They all were allowed one phone call. Terrance was unable to make contact with his parents by phone, so he asked one of his cellmates who made contact with his mother to try and alert his parents for him. The four men sat in the cell after making their calls reflecting on how they got into this situation. Terrance was in shock because this happened to him before. He came out of his developing depression when one of his friends noticed the echo effect in the cell and starting singing the song "Old Man River." The others laughed and began to join in. An old redneck man in another cell yelled at them to "shut the hell up!!" That made the group sing louder as they began to laugh. Finally a police officer walked into the cell block and closed the vault door attached to their cell on them. When they woke in the morning, the group was transported to the local court house where they were placed in a large waiting area with twenty five or thirty other men who were waiting to be seen by a judge. Terrance and the others were hungry as they had not eaten since the night before. They were complaining about their hunger when a cart was rolled into the area with what appeared to be hamburgers and Kool

Aid. Terrance examined the burger and decided that he couldn't eat it. It was so hard that he thought if he dropped it that it would bounce. Terrance drank several cups of Kool Aid in the hope that the liquid breakfast would fill him up. It didn't work, but it was the best he could do to fill up his stomach considering his present circumstances. While waiting for their case to be called another man was led into the room by two extremely large state police officers. This white man was pasty pale. He looked like he had not been in the sun in months. He was about 100 lbs. with a bald head and a close cut salt and pepper beard. The officers took the handcuffs and shackles off him and left the room. He looked around and decided to sit down on the bench right next to Terrance who was sitting alone, fighting depression and wondering whether or not his parents had been contacted. The white man pulled out a pouch of tobacco and some tops paper, and then began to roll himself a cigarette. He asked Terrance in a deep southern drawl what he was locked up for? Terrance told him the whole story, never noticing that everyone else had moved to other side of the room. Terrance looked across the room at his friends who motioned to him to come sit with them. He didn't understand the urgency of their request until he asked the pale man what he did to get locked up. In that same deep drawl the man told him he was on trial for killing sixteen people in Florida. Terrance couldn't believe that he was talking to a mass murderer. He didn't want to appear scared after getting this information although his heart began to beat fast. Now he wanted to ease away from this guy gracefully. He didn't want him to know he was moving away from him because he was a murderer and he didn't want to be victim seventeen. Terrance was bailed out of making a decision when someone came into the room and called his case. The four men were not taken into a court room. Instead they were led into the judge's chambers, where they were introduced to an attorney who told them he was there to represent them. He didn't ask them their side of the story or any other questions. The judge came into the room from what appeared to be his private bathroom dressed in a long black robe. He was an overweight white man who must have weighed three hundred pounds. He told all four men to sit down on the sofas in the room and then as he sat down he said, "Now why are you boys here." He further told them that he had reviewed the police report and wanted to hear their side of the story. Terrance volunteered to speak for the group as he explained why they took the television shell from in front of the store, and why they did not think that they were doing anything wrong. The judge leaned back in his chair behind his desk, thought for a second and then said that although they may have thought the television was trash they didn't get permission from the store owner to take the property. He then ordered bail in the amount of one hundred dollars each. On the way back to the jail they found out that they only had to pay a bail bondman twenty five on the one hundred dollar bail. To their surprise when they arrived back at the jail they were informed that a representative from the school was on his way to bail them out. They were given back the street clothes and placed in a holding cell until they were released about an hour later. When the four were walking out of the prison one of the redneck guards said to them "You niggers will be back!" Terrance looked back at him once he cleared the outside door and said "The hell we will!" On the ride back to the campus the group found out that the school had a dean whose job it was to get students out of jail. He explained to them that this type of thing happens to students all of the time. He also told them that their families had wired the money for each of them to be released. Terrance's parents believed his story but were disappointed that he didn't act smarter in this situation especially since he had just recently had another bout with the police. The charges for this crime were eventually dropped on all four students. They subsequently found out, that not only was the value of the TV shell only twenty five dollars but that one of the arresting officers, the store owner, the judge and the bail bondsman were all part of the same family. They had a racket going setting up people, "mostly blacks", by charging them with a crime, setting bail, and then dropping the charges. The percentage of bail money paid was a fee for the bondsman's services.

As a result of Terrance's arrests and the abuse and humiliation he suffered he found himself taking a more radical stance on politics. He began to think that change had to be forced on the more conservative thinking people, be they black or white. In the late 1960s FAMU was beginning to, like so many other traditionally black colleges, challenge the status quo. The older more established faculty members wanted to preserve the good old days where the model of conformity was the same as the white schools. This however was quickly becoming the time of big afro hair styles, bell bottom pants, free love, drug use and black is beautiful. "Power to the people" was the motto and a clinched fist was the greeting by black men. To see someone in African dress was not uncommon. You might not have been a Muslim but you still read the Muhummad Speaks Newspaper, and whenever you could you would listen to speechs by Malcolm X or Stokley Carmichael. After Dr. King's death it was much easier to convince young progressive thinking people that maybe their previous thought process needed to change. Terrance was one of those converts.

Radical and progressive thinking students did not want to accept slowly progressive change. They felt the time for change was now. When Terrance entered the University all freshman male students were required to take Army ROTC for one year. They were issued army uniforms which they had to wear one day a week on the day that they took military classes. Terrance hated this requirement. He knew guys from his neigborhood that went into the service but that was the furthest thought from his mind. On one occasion all the students in the ROTC program about, 800 strong, had to line up in formation on the football field as the school was expecting an army general to come and inspect the troops. Terrance thought to himself this was like being in the damn army for real. The uniform of the day was dress greens. This uniform was not made to be worn in 90 degree weather. Time passed as everyone stood at parade rest. The sun was beaming down and everyone was sweating. Almost two hours into standing on the field the word came down that the genaral's helicopter was delayed. To make things worse many students, male and female including Billy had gathered in the stands and were teasing everyone standing on the field. "Hey you dumb asses you look hot. Want a drink of water? What time are you leaving for Viet nam," is what Terrance heard. He wanted to give them the finger but thought he would be singled out for punishment if he got caught, so he just laughed at the jokes like everyone standing there with him. Suddenly out the corner of his eye Terrance saw one of the students stagger out of the formation turn around and collapse on the ground. An ambulance, which had been standing by, pulled up to the student who was given water and removed out of the sun and away from the parade grounds. Terrance watched intensely how he was treated. He saw that after he recovered he was sent packing. Terrance thought "shit everyone out here on this football field could be suffering from heat stroke. Why am I out here, other than to get a grade. I don't need an "A" in war a "C" will do; it's passing. With those thoughts in mind, Terrance grabbed his head, staggered off the line, let his eyes roll up in his head, spun around and fell to the ground. He deserved an academy award for his performance. He did receive the same response as the fellow who fainted before him. Maybe the guy who fell, thought of fainting first or maybe he wasn't pretending. Terrance didn't care all he wanted to do was get off that hot ass field and out of the sun. Billy told Terrance later that after his fainting spell soldiers started dropping like flies. They were dropping so fast that the medics couldn't handle them all. The general never arrived leaving 800 black men standing on a hot field for hours. "Go army!!" These types of incidents were common and were the types of traditional events that the more progressive students wanted to change. Over the next few months negotiations between the President of the University, the board of directors, and the students elected to represent the student body. Terrance was elected to sit in on one of these meetings. Issues like offering more black studies courses and the mandatory ROTC program were discussed. These meetings ended in a stalmate. Meetings were subsequently held among the students and it was decided to make a statement by taking over the administration building. This tactic had been used on several other campuses. Terrance was reluctant to get involved in this type of activity. He was afraid of being kicked out of school; but the more he heard about what he considered to be crazy and out dated traditions in the school the more he realized that he should take a stand. He was selected to be head of the food committee as the students expected to be in the building for an indefinite time. His small committee happened to be young men, who thought like criminals when the reason for doing so surfaced. One the group members told Terrance that every night the local supermarket had bread, donuts, milk, eggs, and juice deliveries at about 3:30 AM. These things were left outside the front doors of the market unprotected. He suggested that they steal the produce for their use since they had no budget for food, plus the store was white owned. The group had ten members and set it up so that two members would approach the store at a time while the other three teams acted as look outs from hidden positions. Each particpant had three pillow cases to fill up. The team decided that the best night to execute this operation was Sunday night as they felt it was the quiet time in town. They all agreed that no one should know what they were doing, and if successful no one outside of the ten of them should know where the food came from, or was hidden, until the event took place. There had been rumors at some of the larger meetings that there were undercover police and FBI agents posing as students on campus.

Terrance had mixed emotions about the operation but he didn't want to seem like a punk, and he rationlized that what he was doing was for a good cause. He had been inside the Tallahassee jail and he didn't want to go back, so the plan had to work. On the night of the plan the group met at 2:30 AM and set out to accomplish their task. One team at a time quickly ran down to the enclosed but unlocked area in front of the supermarket. After ascertaining that the food was there, the first team signaled the others. Terrance and his partner were the last to go. He reached the store front, palms sweating, heart beating a mile minute. He did feel less anxious once he put his hands in a crate which was in a dark area and felt boxes of what turned out to be donuts and bread. He was glad that his comrades who preceeded him to the spot got the milk, juice, and the heavier items. He filled up his three pillow cases and escaped. As he crossed the street he heard one of the look outs yell "police!!" Terrance took off running as fast as he could toward a wooded area near by. He thought that if he could reach that area he could avoid the police. While running he heard what appeared to be at least two shots. They weren't firing at him but he ran low to the ground, as his street instincts suggested, making himself as small of a target as possible. Once he got to the wooded area, which was a pre-planned escape route he saw police search lights scanning the area. Terrance moved in a direction away from the lights. He knew that some of the other participants in the caper had also planned to escape through the woods so he hoped they wouldn't lead the cops to him. Terrance reached a place in the woods where he felt safe and where he could see anyone coming from any direction. He didn't see any police lights, so decided to wait it out where he was. He waited a couple hours before deciding to head back to the rendezous spot, before the sun came up. When he arrived there everyone else was there waiting for him except a student named Blue. His partners in crime told him that Blue had been shot by the police when he was running away with his loot. He made it back to the rendezvous, spot but was in such bad shape that he was taken to the hospital where he was immediately arrested because he had a gunshot wound. When Terrance told them that he layed low in the woods for 2 hours they all fell out laughing. Someone told him they were worried that he got shot also. The group felt sure that Blue would not rat out the rest of the group. He grew up in the south. He was tough and he knew how to handle himself around redneck cops. The group immediately contacted a lawyer who was sympathetic to their cause. This lawyer was able to get Blue a nominal bail since he had no prior arrests, and the police did not find any of the stolen merchandise on him. His only real crime was running from the cops and getting shot. The next day there was an article in the local news paper concerning a robbery at the supermarket. Terrance went to see Blue in the hospital after the police were no longer guarding his room. He smiled when he recognized the undercover cops who were watching Blue's room to see who visited him. They were so obvious that they might as well have kept on their police uniforms. Blue told Terrance that the cops were just starting to lean on him physically when the lawyer who represented him showed up. They were pissed off when he told them that he wasn't going to tell them shit. They threatened to kill him and get rid of his body. Hearing Blue's story, Terrance thought to himself that the police were willing to kill a black over some donuts and milk. They also told Blue that they were the police and they had the power to do what they wanted! Blue said they got even angrier when the lawyer showed up and stopped their interrogation. The last thing they told Blue was that his "Uppity nigger ass" was going to be theirs once he hit the street again. Since Blue was shot in the back shoulder, and there was no evidence that he participated in any crime, he was given a bail of $200 which was paid by the student organization.

The day of the take over arrived. Fifty students were positioning themselves to be the first wave to enter the building. Terrance and his group were assigned to be in the second wave as they had the food and other things such as medical supplies and flash lights. His group was standing directly across the street from the administration building when Terrance noticed that there was a large amount of construction work going on, much more than usual, much more than he had seen since he entered the school. Someone pointed out that there were also a hell of a lot of construction workers for what appeared to be a small job. As the group waited for the green light, Billy and a couple other guys came over to the leaders of the first wave and told them to call it off. Members of the group detected that the FBI and local police had been advised of the take over. Terrance and his group were angry but happy at the same time. Rumor later had it that the construction workers were FBI agents and undercover police officers, who were prepared to act when the student assaulted the administration building. The ten members of the group, who stole the food split it up among themselves after the operation was called off.

Billy and Terrance had never eaten so many donuts in all of their lives. The leadership in the take over group now knew that there was an informant on campus. They discussed who they thought the traitor might be and came up with a list of several possible names. They then set out one by one to see who set them up and took the bait. On one occasion the word was leaked that some students were going to rob a jewelry store and use the proceeds to finance another try at taking over the administration building. On another occasion it was leaked that a shipment of brown heroin was going to be available to buy for the right price. Although none of the events took place, the group figured out who the informant was. His name was Jerry, and he was actually a Tallahassee police officer. He grew up in Tallahassee, so no one suspected him of being the police. It was determined although never proven that he was probably recruited right out of the police academy to work undercover so no one, even the locals knew him to be a cop. This was common practice among police forces across the country during this period of time as radical groups were springing up everywhere. When Terrance was given this information he thought about how he had seen Jerry at all of the meetings. He didn't seem to fit in with other group members and appeared to be a bit older than most of them. He never said anything and many times was one of the last people to leave the meetings. A plan was put into motion to deal with him. Terrance nor Billy wanted to know the details of the plan because they knew it might result in his being seriously harmed. They talked about it and then felt that they could better serve the organization by being activists in the public eye. They weren't killers, and they knew it. The word got out around campus that Jerry disappeared. Both Terrance and Billy were questioned by the police, but had no information for them. Several weeks later Jerry reappeared. After he reappeared he was never seen on campus again. Terrance ran into him in the downtown area once and he had visible scars on his face from what appeared to have been a severe beating. During their encounter they just greeted each other briefly and then went their separate ways. There was another person who was targeted as an informant but after Jerry's disappearance she dropped out of the student organization.

Over a period of time and through more meetings with the school's board of directors, who now began to understand what extremes the students were willing to go to for change, became more willing to compromise for the good of the school and it's reputation. Terrance felt a sense of accomplishment the first time he heard a Malcolm X recording being played over a loud speaker from the administration building. He thought to himself "I helped do that."

CHAPTER 4

"TIME FOR LOVE"

Terrance felt that he had accomplished a lot for a freshman, but he had neglected his love life. He and Sheila were still communicating, but it was now a long distance romance, and she was planning on attending Howard University and not come to Florida. He had sexual encounters, but nothing lasting. They were all beautiful but nothing clicked. He really hadn't thought much about a relationship, as he was fixated on other matters. Women were simply a sexual release. Over the summer Terrance and Sheila saw each other, but in the fall they went their separate ways. He went back to Florida, and she went to Washington DC. Terrance now was thinking more about a more meaningful relationship with someone of the opposite sex. The fact that Billy had been in a relationship for some time re-enforced his feelings about finding someone. He felt that he didn't have time to play the field. That took too much work. The two men were living together and so they spent hours talking about many issues, including women. Billy seemed to be attracted to older women or maybe they were attracted to him. His current girlfriend was four years older than he, but that didn't seem to affect them. Her name was Barbara, a beautiful light skinned woman with jet black long hair down to her behind. She had previously been married, and after her divorce decided to go to college. During one of their many conversations that she shared with Terrance she told him that her father was a successful drug dealer in Miami Florida. She further shared that he had never been arrested for drugs, he wasn't a street level dealer and that she didn't find out what he did for a living until she was in her late teens. She only knew him to be a loving family man before she discovered what he did. Barbara didn't use drugs, but she knew how to hook you up if you wanted something. Barbara did turn Terrance on to a few of her girlfriends, but he wasn't turned on by any of them, mentally or physically. Terrance thought about what he wanted in a woman. Billy kept telling him to be flexible. Terrance knew he didn't want a lady friend who was cynical. He had met women he would describe that way. He felt that cynical women were usually angry women. Angry women, he felt, tended to take out their anger on the person closest to them. This was usually their man. He thought, show me an angry woman and you will see a woman who spends most of her time alone. No matter how good she was in between the sheets, no man wants to deal with a woman who is angry all the time. She could be about spending his money or, she might not be the most attractive female on the planet, a man will deal with her, maybe even fall in love. If she is mad about something most of the time black men will instinctively stay away from her. A woman who appears to have serious issues no matter how fine she is, most men will stay away from. When he was in his early teens and saw a good looking older woman without a man he wondered why. Now he would think to himself she's probably angry or has issues. He definitely didn't want a woman who was looking to start a family. He had too many things that he wanted to accomplish. Children weren't in the mix, and he didn't want his children growing up without a father. He wasn't raised that way. He wouldn't mind having a religious woman as long as she used religion not as a crutch, but as a support system. He saw that quality in his mother who never walked around her home preaching or praising God. She did however, seem to practice in her everyday life what the bible taught. Terrance admired, respected, and related to these qualities in her, as did most of his friends.

Then there was Mary. She was an army brat who lived in Columbia Georgia. She came down to visit FAMU in her senior year of high school with plans of attending the school in the fall. She was proud, walked like a queen, and proud of her African heritage. Terrance was immediately attracted to her beautiful chocolate brown skin. Her natural hairstyle was cut short to fit her pretty round face. He was always attracted to dark skin women, but they never seemed to be attracted to him. Once he had a conversation with her about blackness and where people of color should be going as race, he was hooked. They met literally by accident. One day Billy and Terrance were driving in the Volkswagon that Billy bought, when they were hit in the rear by a woman driving another car. This woman was a student at A. & M. Mary was a passenger in the car. The damage was minimal, but while Billy and the woman driver were exchanging information, Terrance and Mary were off to the side in their own conversation. It was obvious that they were attracted to each other, but because of the circumstances of the meeting Terrance thought it inappropiate to pursue romance. As luck would have it the two met again later the same evening at a party. Once he saw Mary at the party, Terrance did not hesitate to take advantage of the opportunity. This was the appropriate time. There were other men at the party who also saw her beauty and zeroed in on her but Terrance felt he had an advantage because he had met her earlier that day. Terrance decided to be aggressive, so he walked up to Mary while she was talking to another man, grabbed her by the hand, and whispered in her ear "Come with me." She didn't resist and followed him. Later when alone, Terrance thought about his past experiences with guys from the south and now understood, why some of them hated the students from the north. His aggressive nature with Mary was one of the reasons why. Their approach was more in the manner of a southern gentlemen. There was nothing wrong with that, but some women preferred bad boys. The two of them went outside from the party and sat in Billy's Volkswagon where they smoked a joint and got to know each other through conversation. Terrance couldn't believe that this young woman was only 17 years old. Her thought process and maturity suggested that she was older. They talked for hours until her friend came looking for her telling her it was time to go. Mary gave Terrance her phone number and told him that if she had any doubts about attending FAMU next year he had erased them. Terrance knew that he was not going to wait til next year to see this woman again. Weeks went by and Terrance couldn't stop thinking about her. He, Billy, another friend named Tony now rented a house off campus. There was no phone in the house like there was when they lived in the dormitory so to make calls meant finding a phone booth. Tony, who was from Baltimore, also had a girlfriend. One night when Terrance was sitting around high and alone, listening to the Marvin Gaye song "I Want You But I Want You To Want Me Too" over and over again, Tony tossed him his car keys and told him to "Go find a phone booth and call that woman." Terrance took the advice hoping the whole time he was driving to the phone booth that Mary was home. He was happy and relieved when she answered the phone. The first thing they both did was to exchange addresses which they didn't do when they first met. If they couldn't talk on the phone they could at least write each other. Terrance was not satisfied with just writing, so he made plans to visit her in Georgia. He told her that he needed to put some money together first so he could pay for a place to stay. This became Terrance's mission, get money to go see Mary. So Terrance went to see one of the school Deans about helping him find a job. This Dean had previously backed him when he got into a physical fight with a guy who challenged him, after he felt that Terrance had taken his girlfriend.

On the night of this incident Terrance danced with this young woman on several occasions. They left the party together where they engaged in some heavy petting, but no sex. The woman never told Terrance that she had a boyfriend and he didn't find that out until at around 2AM when her boyfriend starting kicking the hell out of his dormitory door while yelling "Open up this door so that I can kick your ass for messing with my girl!!" Terrance was half asleep and coming down off of a high, so he decided to ignore this knucklehead who was obviously drunk, but the guy wouldn't let up, banging on the door. Billy looked over at Terrance after 15 minutes of banging and said "Please go out there and kick his ass so I can get some sleep. Terrance aggravated now, put on his pants opened the door and said lets go outside and settle this. He didn't feel like explaining what he did earlier. The guy was drunk and probably wouldn't have heard him anyway. By now everybody on the floor in the dorm was awake because of the banging and was looking for a fight night. Terrance walked out of the building with his adversary following. Once outside Terrance turned to the guy who had been mouthing off all the way out of the building, and without saying a word punched him in the face. The big mouth went down to the ground, but sprung back to his feet throwing up his hands to defend himself. He swung at Terrance who moved away from his punches, and countered by hitting him several more times. Terrance observed that his opponent appeared to be a strong country boy. He knew that if this guy was able to grab him and throw him to the ground he could win the battle so he used the Muhammad Ali tactics of stick and move. Terrance hit the guy so many times that he was surprised at how much punishment he could take. Terrance could hear the crowd yelling oohs and aahs with every punch he placed on the guys face. Blood was everywhere. None of it belonged to Terrance. Finally he gave the guy an out by saying "Have you had enough?" He was also giving himself an out as he was tired as hell from punching on this man. This enraged the guy and he charged at Terrance one more time. Terrance reared back and put everything into his punch landing squarely on his opponent's nose and knocking him out in the process. The crowd surrounded Terrance as if he had won a championship fight. Billy splashed water on his face and said "Now come on, let's go get some sleep!"

The next day Terrance was summoned to the office of the Dean of men, Dean Bailey. The Dean was a childhood friend of Billy's father. He also was from New York. After hearing about the fight, he wanted to hear Terrance's side of the story. Terrance was aware of the association the Dean had with his roommate's father, so he was relaxed when walking into the Dean's office. They shook hands, and after Terrence was seated he explained what happened. After hearing the story the Dean shared with Terrance that he already had heard that he didn't start the fight, in fact, tried to avoid it. He seemed to have admired how Terrance handled himself, without condoning the fight. He told him, off the record, that he heard that he kicked the guy's ass. Terrance responded, while smiling, that you can't live in Philly without knowing how to hold your hands. Translation: Philly boys know how to box. He then shared a story that happened to him which cured him of being afraid to fist fight.

When Terrance reached junior high school there were a number of bullies who picked on the new 7th graders. The bullies were older and organized in their attacks. They messed with kids during lunch periods, in between classes, and after school. Terrance was chased home on several occasions, even then using his speed to avoid injury. On one of those occasions five bullies were chasing him home where one of the gang happened to be just as fast as he was, and almost caught him as he reached his front door. Terrance slammed the door behind himself so hard that the glass in the door broke. It just so happened that his father was home that particular day. He heard the glass break and ran downstairs to see what happened. Terrance never told his father about the problem with the bullies. He figured that since he wasn't the one it would eventually stop. He also didn't want his father think that he was scared. He told his dad what happened, after which his father looked outside and saw that his son's pursuers were still there. He then turned back to his son and told him that the only way to get the gang to leave him alone was to go outside and fight them all! Terrance thought to himself "is he out of his mind, me against five 8th and 9th graders. They will kill me. His father saw his apprehension and told him, you won't have to fight them all at once. I will see to that, but you got to fight them. After that statement he picked up a baseball bat that Terrance had in the down stairs closet, went outside where he told the gang that his son was coming out to fight them one at a time. They agreed to the terms. Terrance's dad came back into the house and said, "Let's go." This wasn't a request this was a command. Terrance was never one to enjoy pain. The sight of blood made him woozy. He told his dad that he didn't want to go out there and fight. His father hesitated for a second, took a deep breath, and then said, "You can either fight them, or fight me, your choice." Terrance looked at this man he had known all of his life and he could tell from his body language that he meant what he said. He figured that the kid's punches would hurt a lot less than those of his dad. He was more afraid of his father than he was of them, so he slowly went outside, scared to death. The gang formed a circle with Terrance in the middle while his dad stood on the outside of the circle holding the baseball bat. Terrance then heard a boy say "Me first!" He was smallest of the five, so Terrance thought that if he beat him up, the others would go away. This kid might have been small but he was quick and had obviously been in his shares of fights as he pelted Terrance with punches so fast that he couldn't even block them all. It seemed to Terrance that he had been fighting for hours when the guy he was fighting, who had been kicking his ass, was tapped on the shoulder by another kid in the circle. He jumped in and the first kid jumped out. Terrance kept looking to dad for help but all he heard from him was "Fight!" By the time Terrance got to the fourth kid he was bleeding from the mouth, and his face felt funny, but he was still alive. He was more tired than hurt. He looked over his shoulder at this point and saw a police car pull up. He was never so happy to see the police. He thought "Whew, this is over," until he watched his father walk over to the policemen whisper something to them, both of whom were black. The cops then leaned against their car and did not say a word. This was a signal to the gang to keep kicking Terrance's ass. He did get in some good shots during the fight especially to the bigger boys as they were slower and easier to hit. Finally the fifth guy decided not to fight. The gang then picked up their belongings and left the scene. Terrance noticed as a couple of them walked away that they were also bleeding. He felt a sense of power seeing the damage he had done to boys that only minutes before he had been scared of. He discovered that he could take a punch to the face and live. Later that evening his father explained to him that he couldn't always avoid problems by running. Sometimes he had to face the problem head on. He heard his parent's arguing after his mother found out what happened, but he knew his father was right. The next day at school Terrance had no problems with the bullies. They moved on to other kids who were untested. He was thankful now that his father made him stand up for himself. Dean Bailey recounted a simular experience in his childhood.

Since Terrance now needed a job to get some money so that he could visit Mary, he decided to make a visit back to see Dean Bailey. He knocked on the Dean's door, and was told to enter, at which time he pled his case for finding employment on campus. He never told the Dean that the real reason he wanted a job was so that he could go and see a girl. At the end of Terrance's speech Dean Bailey told him that it seemed like he wanted a position not a job. Nevertheless, he got Terrance a job, in of all places, one of the female dorms. Terrance thought he had died and gone to heaven. He spend two hours a day in the female dormitory changing light bulbs, sweeping the hallway floors, and talking to women who many times would come out of their rooms in their panies and bras acting surprised when they heard the warning yelled "man on the floor." It wasn't what he wanted to do for a living but he could do anything on a temporary basis. He never thought he would be a maintenance man, hell that is why he decided to stay in college after failing to make the team, so that he wouldn't end up doing manual labor to make a living. Whenever he thought about sweet Mary he was motivated. He finally saved up enough money to make the weekend trip. He took a bus to Columbia where Mary met him at the bus station. She drove him in her mother's car to a local motel and told him to get settled, and that she would be back later to pick him up. She returned later that evening and took him to meet her parents who appeared to be good and reasonable people. Terrance enjoyed talking to Mary's mother as he remembered some advice his father gave him years before when he first developed an interest in girls. "Always check out the mother of the girls you date because that is probably who those girls will be in later years." If Mary ends up like her mother, who besides having a positive personality was also very attractive, she would be alright, Terrance thought. They left Mary's house after her family dinner, telling her parents that they were going to a movie. They both knew that story was a lie. Instead they headed straight back to Terrance's motel room. On the way to the motel they stopped at a liquor store and bought a couple of bottles of Boones Farm Apple Wine. When they reached the motel room Terrance wasted no time trying to set the mood for romance. He dimmed the lights, located the black radio station, and poured two glasses of wine over ice. He was about to light a joint when Mary came out of the bathroom completely nude. Her body was so perfect that Terrance forgot about lighting up. She smiled at him and asked him if he liked what he saw? He nodded yes. She then asked him to just look for a few minutes not touch. Terrance had never been asked this before by a woman, but he had no problems following her instructions; besides this just gave him time to fire up a joint. The night was enjoyable for the couple. Before Mary left the hotel room, around 2AM, she kissed Terrance on the cheek and told him that she made the request to look and not touch for a few minutes, because she wanted him to become more visually stimulated so that she could get the full affect of his masculine powers. They spent the rest of the weekend socializing with Mary's friends and making love. Terrance went back to FAMU with a new attitude.

A couple of months later Terrance invited Mary to visit as he and his roomates purchased tickets to see the singing group the Temptations. On the night of the event the three couples sat around the rented house smoking reefer and drinking wine in anticipation of listening to good music. They talked about what time they should leave for the concert as they didn't want to miss a note of the music. Billy's girlfriend talked about how Terrance had changed since he met Mary. She told the group that he was no longer grumpy. Terrance defended himself by saying he had a militant attitude, not a grumpy attitude. The time was 5PM and the concert started at 7, so they all thought they had an hour to continue getting high and talking before leaving. Billy and Tony were feeling good as they kept rolling joint after joint for the group to smoke. The smell of African Musk Incense filled the room, which was lit only by a psychedelic black lamp. Terrance sat on a bean bag chair with Mary sitting between his legs. He felt no pain, as he thought about how lucky he was to have a nice woman sitting in his lap, a nice high, and surrounded by good company. He was so contented that he fell off to sleep. When he woke up he looked around the room and everyone else was also sleep. He slowly looked up at a clock on the wall. When his eyes cleared and he focused in on the clock mounted on the wall the time was 9:40PM. He jumped up rolling Mary to the floor and yelled, "Wake up we missed the concert if that is the right time" pointing to the clock. One by one they all woke up looked at the clock on the wall, wiped their eyes, checked their watches, and realized that they all got so high that they missed the concert of the year. Billy's girlfriend Barbara, who had never gotten high before, but decided to try it since everyone else in the room was smoking and it seemed to be harmless spoke first. "See this is why I never smoked marajuana. It made us all null and void." The group got hostile and told her to sit the hell down. Everyone knew that they had missed out on something nice. Terrance knew that he lost money that he couldn't afford to lose. Billy knew that he was going to hear Barbara's mouth about smoking reefer. He quickly thought about the lecture he knew was coming and he said, well since we missed the concert we might as well make the best of a bad situation, let's smoke the rest of this bag of reefer. Everybody laughed. Barbara gave him a look of disbelief.

Mary and Terrance continued to see each other over the next year, as Terrance continued to involve himself with radical groups on campus, who wanted change now. One of his groups was instrumental in getting the first African Studies Courses added to the school curriculum. When Mary got to FAMU the next year she and Terrance decided to take one of these courses together. The first day of the class, a white man walked into the room. He was about 125 lbs. soaking wet 5'4", wearing bell bottom jeans and sandals with a full red beard. His dress was the total opposite of most of the faculty. He introduced himself as the black studies professor. Terrance looked around the room and saw that the rest of the class was as shocked as him.They never expected to learn African American History from a white man. He started off the lecture by telling the class that he was going to talk today about "Rock throwing, rabbit killing, humans who once roamed the earth!" By the end of the lecture he had the class in his spell. Terrance learned something else during that class, that he hadn't thought about for some time. There are many avenues for learning, even from skinny white men, with red beards. The word quickly got around campus about this teacher who eventually became one of the most popular professors on campus. Once some of the radical groups ascertained that he could be trusted he was even invited to some of their meetings. Terrance thought that over a period of time, rather than the staff changing the students, the students were changing the staff. Everyone seemed to benefit.

CHAPTER 5

"A TIME FOR CHANGE"

Terrance continued his militant stance which got him into trouble occasionally with the local police, who watched the groups he was involved with. On one occasion he received a money order from his grandmother, which needed to be cashed at a bank. He walked to downtown Tallahassee and cashed the money order. Upon leaving the bank he needed some school supplies, so he subsequently crossed the street to go into a store that he knew had what he wanted. When he reached the other side of the street he was stopped by a policeman on a motor cycle. He remembered this officer as one of the ones that treated him roughly when Billy and he got arrested. Terrance instantly got an attitude as the officer told him that he was being cited with a ticket for jay walking in the middle of the block. The police officer began writing the ticket while lecturing him about how much money the city spends a year on white lines at the corners of each street so that pedestrians can cross safely. Terrance felt this was just a form of racial harassment. He had seen white people in the past come out of the bank and cross the street in the same area without any problems from the police. Consequently he interrupted the speech by saying in an angry tone "Man if you are going to give me a ticket, just give me the ticket, I don't want to hear a sermon!" The police officer after hearing that made a call on his radio using code and a deep southern drawl. Within minutes three police cars pulled up to the scene. The cops got out of their vehicles and with the assistance of the motor cycle cop pushed Terrance against one the police car and handcuffed him. Terrance couldn't believe he was being arrested for jay walking and he told the cops so. He further stated as he was being pushed into a cop car that he had a constitutional right to speak his mind even to the police. He told the cops that giving a police officer back talk was not against the law. The two cops in the front seat didn't say a word but drove to the local precinct and once again literally threw him into a cell. Terrance had flash backs of his last encounter with this jail. He couldn't believe that he was back there again. He now remembered what Billy told him about rules in the south. An hour after he was sitting in the cell a police officer came to him and told him he would be released if he could pay the twenty dollar fine for jay walking. When Terrance was brought into the jail his property was taken which included seventy five dollars in cash. He had just cashed a money order in the bank, so he told the officer to let him have his property and he would pay the fine. The officer refused to give him his property. He was told that he couldn't be given his things until he was released. Terrance knew what they were up to now, so he asked for his one phone call which they allowed. He called Mary, who was in her dormitory room on campus and asked her to come down and pay his fine which she did.

Terrance knew that the cops wanted to keep him in jail as long as possible, so they wouldn't let him pay the fine out of the money he had in his property. As he left the jail with Mary he heard a cop say, "That'll teach that nigger a lesson bout messin with us!"

When Terrance got back to school he told his friends what happened to him with the police. The news of what happened spread quickly through the campus. Barbara, who was a journalism major, and who worked for the campus newspaper got Terrance to agree to an interview. She knew that he would be passionate when telling his story. The article was printed in the paper along with a photo of Terrance. There was an immediate reaction to the story by the student body. Groups on campus joined together and decided to march to the police precinct in protest against how Terrance was treated. Terrance was in total agreement with this move. Hell he was now famous and he loved it. The word of what happened spread across to Florida State University, also located in Tallahasee, where the radical white group SDS (students for a democratic society) wanted to join in the protest. Some of the prelaw students filed the paperwork to get a permit to march, so that the police could not arrest the marchers for an illegal assembly. Many of them knew what to do after they had marched with Martin Luther King Jr. As quickly as the word spread throughout the campus it also spread to the faculty. Terrance was then contacted by Dean Bailey who wanted to meet with him and the University President. He agreed to the meeting because Dean Bailey had always been cool with him. His only stipulation was that he be able to bring Billy along to watch his back. The meeting was set. When Billy and

Terrance arrived at the office of the University President they were escorted into his office like dignitaries. They sat at the end of a long conference table and were greeted by Dean Bailey and the President. They were offered coffee, tea, or soft drinks, but they declined the offer. Terrance thought that they should have offered them some hard liquor. He felt that they were all men who had the power from the people they represented to negotiate. There was some small talk for a few minutes and then the President spoke. He told Billy and Terrance that he thought that it was a bad idea to protest against the police department. He went on to say that he thought that what happened to Terrance was a terrible thing but he had known people who experienced even worse abuse from the police, but chose not to react for the sake of many. Terrance responded by telling the President that he was not one of those people. He further stated that what he was doing was for the greater good of the people. Terrance and his friend left the meeting not compromising on any aspect of the march. When they were leaving the building Billy told Terrance that they should both expect some backlash from the school for their stance. Terrance said "Yeah now we have the Tallahasse Police Department, and the University Adminstration pissed off at us. We must be doing something right."

A few days before the march Terrance and Mary were in his bedroom studying when they heard what sounded like a series of gun shots. When they opened the bedroom door and ran into the living room they saw two bullet holes in a wall and glass on the floor from a broken window. One of the neighbors heard the shots and called the police. When they arrived they inspected the damage and asked a few questions such as "Do you know of anyone who wants to do you harm?" Terrance told him yeah you! They pretended not to know what he was talking about but he was sure that they knew the whole story. The cops searched the area, talked to a few neighbors, took a report, and left. Before they left, Billy pulled up to the house and was informed of what had happened. After they left Billy told Terrance that he going to buy himself a pistol for protection cause the shit was getting serious. He urged Terrance and Tony to do the same. The next day Billy brought home a shinny new Smith and Wesson 38 caliber pistol.

The march started by the adminstration building where there were a few speeches and then proceeded downtown toward the police precinct. The police were waiting for what appeared to be about a thousand students black and white. As they marched downtown Terrance thought back to the KKK march he had witnessed on the same route as this march. He also saw some of the same policemen who had been involved in his two arrests. This time some of them were in plainclothes, but everyone knew they were cops. If they thought they were supposed to be undercover they did a poor job of it. Terrance was not acutely aware of the danger, even though someone had fired a few shots into his home only days before. There were men assigned to watch out for his safety. He didn't see any guns but he was sure some of them were carrying. He found out later that Billy had something to do with that decision. Once the crowd reached the podium Terrance and Mary were escorted up the stairs and given seats on the stage along with several other people including the student body president, members of the local clergy, and the heads of the three major fraternities on campus Omega Psi Phi, Kappa Alpha Psi, and Alpha Phi Alpha. Terrance thought to himself after looking out at a sea of people, most of whom were there to support his cause, that this was one of the most important days in his life. The pride that he felt was indescribable. He also saw in the crowd people who he was sure were law enforcement. Their sun glasses and crew cut hair cuts made them easy to spot among the afro's and long hair. Barbara and Mary had helped Terrance write the speech that he was going to give. He had gone over it a thousand times with their help so he felt ready. When it was Terrance's time to speak he was introduced and then asked to approach the podium. He walked to the podium and before speaking he got a sense of what Dr. King must have felt when he spoke at the March on Washington, several years before. He looked out over the sea of people there to support him and his cause and felt a sense of pride. Just seeing the crowd re-enforced his feeling that he was doing the right thing. Terrance spoke about the injustices against black people that he had seen in Florida since coming to school. He described in detail what happened to him the last time he was taken into custody. How humiliating and brain numbing that experience was for a young black man who never had any past problems with the law. He told the crowd how helpless Billy and he felt when they got arrested. "It wasn't the arrest itelf that bothered him the most, because he knew he was innocent, but the way he was manhandled during the arrest, when he put up no resistance," he told all that came to hear him. He told the crowd that he was taking a stand not only for himself, but for everyone there in attendance. Although there were well over a couple of thousand people in attendance, what Terrance noticed most of all in the crowd were the facial expressions of the cops. They looked like they wanted to pull him off the stage and lynch him from the nearest tree right on the spot. It was at that moment that Terrance realized the danger that he was in. He was now glad for the body guards. He wondered what type of protection he would get after the Rally? None the less now was the time to speak his mind. Upon completion of his speech Terrance received a rousing applause from the crowd. Mary walked to the podium and hugged him so hard he thought she would break his ribs. Terrance was on cloud nine at the end of the rally but he couldn't help but think about the danger he might be in as a result of his speech. He had previously heard stories about brothers who defied the southern system and who eventually disappeared. Black Muslims who lived on campus or in the surrounding area, offered him protection but their goal was to recruit him into the organization which he didn't want to do. Billy and Tony wanted him to buy himself a gun but he thought that if he was caught with a concealed weapon this would play into the hands of the cops. They were looking for a reason to arrest or kill him, preferably the latter. He decided after talking with Mary, who was now even more militant, consequently convincing him that he should take up the study of marshal arts. She told him that he would take the self defense classes with him. Terrance excelled in the classes very quickly. He was athletic and motivated because he feared for his life. He told the instructors that he was not interested in obtaining any of the belts associated with progress in learning to defend himself. A black or brown belt meant nothing to him. He just wanted to be able to kick someone's ass if they messed with him. Fortunately for him he didn't have to use his skills in the weeks and months that would come.

It did come a time when he had to use what he was taught. In his senior year Terrance was assigned to student teach at a white high school located in Tallahassee. He was also allowed to work with the football team as an assistant coach. One day after practice followed by a coaches meeting he was on his way back to his car when he was approached by four white men in plain clothes. They surrounded him in the school parking lot, and one of them told him that they remembered him as being the nigger who caused problems for the Tallahassee police force. He further stated that one of the cops who got into trouble was his brother, who eventually lost his job because of too many complaints of police brutality. "My brother's job was to keep you niggers in line," he blurted out through his rage. He told Terrance that he was now going to pay for what happened to his brother. Terrance immediately dropped the papers in his hands and positioned his body so that his back was against his car. He looked around the parking lot area for help, but there was none. Shit I'm on my own, he thought. Although the sun was beginning to set, Terrance was able to see his assailants, none of which appeared to be holding any guns. If one of them had a gun, he would have been Terrance's first target, because he would have been the deadliest threat. If they all had guns, he knew he was screwed. The next most deadly threat, Terrance thought, was the guy that did the talking. He sensed from this man's voice and his body language that he intended on hurting him badly. He also noticed that he was holding a bat in his hand, at his side. Since marshal arts training taught you to defend yourself against attackers, Terrance waited for his assailants to make their moves. He lowered himself into a bladed combat stance while watching all four men. The man with the bat attacked first holding the bat over his head. He swung the bat hitting Terrance's car as the student teacher moved smoothly to the side avoiding the bat and striking the man on the back of the neck with his fist. He then pinned the man to the car as he kicked the next guy who approached him in the throat. Terrance then rolled across the hood of his car while grabbing the bat out of the hands of the man who attacked first. The third man tried to grab him as he went across the hood but Terrance hit him in the head with the bat that he now had in his possession. The fourth man ran around the car followed by the man who previously held the bat. He moved to avoided being hit with the bat Terrance was swinging as the other man jumped on Terrance's back forcing him to drop the bat. Terrance then flipped this man over his left shoulder as he dropped to his knees striking him first in the face and then in the throat. He then sprang to his feet just in time to block the flailing arms and fists of the man who avoided the bat. He grabbed one of the man's arms as he threw a punch, turned around bringing the man's arm over his shoulder. He then pulled the arm down dislocating it at the elbow. He had practiced this particular move many times, so practice made perfect. He now had disabled three of the four men and while they were trying to recover Terrance jumped in his car and drove away. While driving, Terrance wondered should he go to the police and report the attack. He realized that the reason for the attack was because of his relationship with the police, so he opted to get advice from school officials, and Mary. Terrance and

Mary by this time had drifted apart as she became more militant and decided to convert to IsIam and become a Black Muslim. Terrance knew himself well enough to know that although he admired the discipline that the Muslim brotherhood exihibited, he liked the taste of pork ribs and bacon too much to give them up along with an occasional joint or two. He understood the health benefits Muslims suggested one would gain from abstinence, and what they considered proper eating habits. He however had a different view point on these subjects. Was alcohol and reefer bad for you? No question. The use of these substances had many negative outcomes, compared to positive ones. Terrance would never allow himself to get pushed into a debate over these issues, he knew that based on commom sense he would lose the argument. However, he would debate anyone about the advantages or disadvantages of eating certain foods, in particular, pork products. Terrance would always start off defending his view point, when debating, with the statement that his grandparents and great aunts and uncles, many of whom were in their eighties ate and still eat pork products. Whether it was because that was all they could afford during their early years or by choice, their diets never changed. Since they were all relatively healthy at their ages Terrance felt that why should he change his diet from the one he was raised on. Being a student of history, he did understand that many African countries because of their Islamic beliefs chose not to eat pork products. He respected a person's religious beliefs but since his belief in God was questionable he wasn't going to allow religious beliefs or arguments, to dictate how he thought and what he felt. He thought that it was more of a moderate position to maintain a well balanced diet not over indulging in anything. His grandmother once told him that too much of anything is unhealthy. He felt with this way of thinking he could enjoy all of what life had to offer without sacrificing. Life was for living not sacrificing he felt. If the sacrifice was for one's family or friends it was the right thing to do. However if the sacrifice was a way of getting into heaven, he couldn't relate. Mary and Terrance had remained friends and from time to time they still made love when they got together and were both in the mood. Mary didn't allow her religion to stop her from getting her freak on occasionally. She suggested that her friend seek the guidance and support of one of his mentors Dean Bailey.

Terrance was able to get his old friend Dean Bailey to accompany him to the local precinct to report the attack. The police officer who took the report acted as though this was the first he heard of what happened but Terrance and the Dean both felt he was already aware of what happened. Upon leaving the precinct Terrance told the Dean that he missed his friend Billy who had been his best advisor on matters such as these. Billy had been killed several months before, after he caught a drug addict robbing his apartment. During the incident that led to his death, Billy beat up the heroin addict and put a gun in his mouth threatening to kill him before he called the police. When the junky was released from jail he got hold of a pistol and bushwacked Billy shooting him in the back. He died several days later from the gunshot wounds. The irony in Billy's death was that he saved the life of this same junkie one time in the past. On a prior occasion the junkie named Detroit Donald, passed out after shooting some heroin in his arm. Billy and Barbara happened to be visiting a friend in the same house at that time. He and another guy, who was also in the house, quickly went into action by carrying the junkie into the kitchen from the bathroom, when they couldn't revive him with water, and slaps to the face. They subsequently took ice cubes out of the freezer, pulled down his pants, and rubbed them on his balls. Donald woke up instantly thanks to their efforts to save him. Terrance and Billy both hated junkie's as much as many, but more than most. They felt that black junkies in particular were a disgrace to the negro race. They had seen them steal from their grandmothers to get high. They understand socio political reasons why so many black men they knew turned to hard drugs, however excuses were like ass holes everyone had one. In Donald's case he couldn't use the poor black man persecuted by the system defense because he was the child of two doctors. He wasn't oppressed, he was a fuck up. Because Terrance thought like that, it made dealing with Billy's death that much harder.

A subsequent investigation into the attack on Terrance determined that someone on the high school staff alerted the assailants that Terrance was a teacher at the school. Two of the four men were arrested and pled guilty to assault, receiving probation for the crime. Terrance wasn't satisfied with the sentences but he remembered what Billy told him years before that southern justice was different for the black man, which was why they had to work to change the system.

CHAPTER 6

"WELCOME TO THE REAL WORLD"

Terrance graduated from college without much problem. He wasn't an "A" student, but did well enough to gain praise from some faculty members as they recognized that the brilliance in a person is not always the grade that a student received. They also placed importance on how the student participated in class and how he or she performed out of the classroom setting. Terrance's parents were extremely proud of their son, their being aware that he entered college with one objective and finished with another. They threw him a graduation party when he returned to Philadelphia. One of his favorite uncles at the party after drinking too much, made a speech. "I want to congratulate my nephew on his success, but I want to point out to him that now that he is entering the world of work where there will be no more two months summer vacations! No more Thanksgiving weekends off! No more Christmas weeks off, and no more sleeping til 11 in the morning cause you don't have a class til

1 in the afternoon! Now go find a good job so that you can pay into Social Security, so that I can get my Social Security check on time, when I retire next year youngster."

Terrance had prepared to be a teacher but after returning home he wasn't sure if that was what he wanted to do. His grandmother told him in her usual spiritual way that everyone has a purpose for being alive. He needed to find his. His mother, who was a teacher, told him that if he wanted to be considered for a teaching position in the fall he needed to make up his mind fast. Since he didn't have any clear direction as to what other careers he wanted to pursue he applied, and was given a teaching post. The only problem was that his assignment was in one of the poorest and dangerous neighborhoods in Philadelphia. He wasn't worried about the danger because he had been through too many perilous situations in the past while in school down south. He felt confident that he could protect himself and do a good job at shaping young minds. He wasn't, however, prepared for the new type of danger that awaited.

Terrance was assigned to teach 10th and 11th grade American History. He welcomed the chance to be able to deviate from the lesson plan given to him and talk to teenagers about Black History and it's relationship to American History. He felt that once a young mind had been educated to understand the history of his race, the better prepared he would be to deal with life, in general. He thought he was going to be a great influence on young minds just as his had been an influence. Those thoughts and dreams were out of the window in his first few days of teaching. This was a new generation of children. Some of their reasoning and thought process was due to their environment, which included laissez faire parenting and lack of direction. Many of these students had no plans for the future or hope of achieving anything positive. Life for many of them was a day to day struggle. Kids grow up fast in the ghetto. Terrance was not prepared for what was in front of him. He didn't grow up in a wealthy neighborhood, but many of his friends, inspite of what they didn't have, dreamed of achieving the things that they wanted out of life. Terrance wasn't much older than many of the students in the school. This made him attractive to many of the beautiful young female students in the school. Some times he would look at a 17 year old female student who was perfectly proportioned and think of Mary when they first met. He wanted to treat his students like they were in college, by allowing open seating in his class rooms. He determined who was there by taking attendence. Around his third day in class he began to realize that all the female students were sitting in the first two rows, while the male students sat in the back of class. Some of the female students would sit in their seats in provocative positions vying for his attention. Terrance thought their eager attitudes were because of their thirst for knowledge. He also thought the boys sat in the back of the room because they were not interested in class, and so they wanted to goof off. He was right about the boys, because he was constantly spending time telling those knuckleheads to quiet down and pay attention. The girls, however, had a different agenda. Terrance was made aware of their agenda by a veteran female teacher, who started off making him aware by saying "Be careful!" She further went on to tell him that she over heard some of the girls talking about him in sexual terms. She told him of past staff members who got caught up in the flesh with female students, consequently ending their young careers. The fact that she thought these young teenage girls found him attractive made him even more interesting. After hearing this from the teacher Terrance's first thought was how stupid could he have been not to have recognized this on his own. If nothing else, he considered himself a thinker. He got passed, feeling stupid, and even a bit angry at himself, and then decided to use the attraction of these students to his advantage. It was time for the hunter to be captured by the game. If it took being eye candy to get some students to learn, so be it; whatever works. Terrance knew that there was a line that he shouldn't cross in dealing with students so he was always careful. His next problem was how did he get through to young black boys who obviously had no interest in school? He became frustrated at times when he couldn't get through to a boy who he knew had talents that he was wasting away. When he had to throw a child out of his class because the teenager was uncontrollable or disrespectful, he took it as a personal failure. He realized after talking with other teachers and his mother that he couldn't save every student but that didn't stop him from trying. Terrance eventually got a reputation in the school as someone not to mess with. Many of the students who didn't want to learn, or at least be respectful of others while sitting in his class stopped attending. Terrance had many talks with school administrators about doing community outreach to get to the children and their families. When talking it sometimes felt as though he was back talking to his old college administrators about change. The only difference was that many of these administrators were white.

Even though they had vast experience as teachers they just didn't seem to understand the complexities of being poor and black. In some cases they didn't seem to care. Terrance reflected back to his days in the same school system. The teachers, for the most part, that he learned the most from were black teachers. They commanded attention in class. It also didn't hurt that if you failed to pay attention your parents were notified. Which was a fate worse than death. This generation of parents if contacted many times seemed to defend their children's negative behavior in school. The school board was impotent in dealing with these situations. This frustrated Terrance even more. He had two experiences that made him seriously reconsider his current career course.

Terrance, as he did as a student teacher in college, was able to work after school as an assistant football coach. He decided to turn his frustrated energy from the class room into what he hoped would be a positive coaching experience. One day after football practice he got into his car to head home after a long day. When he reached the corner of the block away from the football field he saw one of his female students named Tisha Smalls waiting for the bus. She had just left cheerleader practice. Besides being attractive Tisha was one of Terrance's brightest students. She was always involved in class discussions, and did well on all her tests. Terrance knew where she lived, from reviewing her school records, as he did all of his students. He rolled down the window of his brand new red Volkwagon and offered her a ride home since he was going right past her street on his way home. She climbed in his car and thanked him for the ride. During the ride they talked about the football team and other topics related to school. When Terrance pulled up in front of her modest row home they continued to talk about school matters. Terrance felt like a real mentor until just before Tisha got out of his car she said," You know Mr. Jackson, we have been sitting here in your car talking for maybe twenty minutes. During that time I have seen my mother look out the window at us at least three times. Do you know that I could get you into serious trouble by saying that you were "Rapping" to me while I was in your car." She turned towards Terrance, smiled, and without saying another word got out of his car. Terrance thought to himself "Oh shit" what have I done now? How could I put myself in this position? Why am I so trusting, he thought to himself? He didn't expect this type of behavior from one of his star students. He didn't drive off right away still in shock over what had just happened. He decided that he shouldn't worry as he hadn't done anything wrong. If he was guilty of anything it was making the stupid decision to drive a female student home. Nothing ever happened to Terrance as result of his encounter with Tisha. She never brought it up again although from time to time he would look at her in class and she appeared to have this sheepist grin on her face. Terrance took no chances of upsetting her. Whenever he got to her test papers, he didn't even check them he just gave her a ninty five to one hundred grade.

One more incident changed Terrance's mind about teaching. He had an ongoing conflict with a 16 year old male student who was constantly disruptive in the classroom, and at times tried to intimidate him because he had gang affiliation. Terrance wasn't intimidated as he threw the kid out of his classroom on a few occasions. He subsequently called for a meeting with the child and his parents. Only the child's father showed up to the meeting as Terrance was informed that the boy's mother was strung out on heroin and was not in the picture. It came out during the meeting how angry that young man was about his situation. Dad, in his attempts to overcome his guilt would always defend or make excuses for his son's behavior. Since there was no corrective actions taken at home to address his behavior, he eventually was kicked out of school. He was then sent to a school for kids with delinquent and behavioral problems. One day after leaving school as Terrance was walking to his car he noticed the 16 year old, who had been kicked out of school, sitting across the street on some steps with his gang. Terrance kept his eyes on them as he approached his car remembering what happened to him when he was a student teacher. He was prepared for anything. He subsequently started up his car, and as he drove away the car began to buck and jerk indicating that something was wrong. Before he drove to the end of the block the car stalled and would not start again. All of the boys who had been sitting on the steps cheered and laughed. Terrance heard someone from the crowd yell "That'll teach your ass!" Terrance had the car towed to the dealer where the next day he found out that sugar had been poured into his gas tank destroying the engine. He was as angry as he had been in a long time. He knew right away who put the sugar in his tank but he couldn't prove it. He felt impotent, helpless, and angry. He reported his suspicions to the police but they couldn't do anything because he had no proof. This was the last straw. He knew that if he didn't change professions he would end up hurting one of those kids. He felt bad about leaving the promising students but this was also about his own mental survival. He admired the teachers who cared and stayed. He needed to find a way of teaching, counseling, and mentoring where he had more control over the individuals he was servicing. He felt that teaching was so regimented, that it made it difficult to help some of the people who needed help the most. Terrance tinkered around with several jobs over the next few years. Most of the jobs were in the field of social work and substance abuse treatment. During these years he ran into people who he knew from the street, who had lost their sense of will to live the good life to drugs. Although Billy's death was constantly on his mind a few years later, he came to the conclusion that the best way to honor his friend was to try and help people like the one who killed him. This direction also gave Terrance a sense of helping the communities like the one he grew up in. Since he had been away from Philly for the better part of four years and away from the drug scene, except for marijuana smokers, for some time, many of those in the drug world were almost like strangers. One day one of his old friends was admitted to the treatment program where he worked. Upon seeing Terrance he said,"End Zone Jackson, I haven't seen you in so long that I thought you were dead." He received similar responses from others he knew back in the day. Terrance felt he was helping to change some people's lives working in a substance abuse program, but he still met with frustration, because even in this profession he didn't have the control over the population he worked with to force them to make the right decisions for themselves. Decisions which were obvious to most people couldn't or wouldn't be made by drug and alcohol addicted people sometimes even with good support systems. He did learn a lot about accepting people where they were mentally, and emotionally, but it hurt him to see so many people, and black people in particular destroy their lives over drugs. He read reports and articles that informed him how the United States Government through covert operations in the 1960's and 70's flooded many black communities in urban areas with drugs as a way of countering the black awareness movement. He believed what he read because he had witnessed, and been a part of the black power movement. He saw how the movement gave people pride in themselves.They were proud of just being black. This pride led people who previously were unmotivated to want to improve themselves. Black people had been on a path of moving up economically and socially for years, but the civil rights, black power movements, helped open doors never open to African Americans before. Terrance felt that drugs froze that growth and took away some peoples motivation to succeed. He hated the government for what he believed was their conspiratorial behavior, towards the black community. When he hated something bad enough he wanted to try and change it. The question was how much could he do? He was still searching for the right career move to achieve this goal. He finally got some ideas on what he was looking for when he decided to move to New York, chasing his future wife.

Camille Nichols was a caramel colored beauty born and raised in New York City. Terrance met her at a party while she was visiting Philadelphia. She was inteligent, educated, and worldly. Everything that he wanted in a woman he found in her. The couple spent several months traveling back and forth between New York and Philly while dating, when Terrance finally decided that he needed a change, so he moved to New York. He liked what he saw there when he was visiting. They married shortly after Terrance relocated. They also bought a co-op apartment in Queens. Camille, who was a teacher, got along fabulously with Terrance's mother who was also a teacher. The two women had that in common.

New York was a place in the mid to late seventies where a person who was ambitious and community minded could do a great deal of good. New York was infested with drug addicts and alcoholics, as were many other major cities, including the city he left. However, Terrance felt he needed a change, so New York now was the place. Since Terrance had some experience in community work and treating drug and alcohol addicted people, finding work was easy for him. While working in a treatment program Terrance met a New York State Parole Officer who came to meet with him and find out how well one of his clients who was also on parole was progressing in the program. During this time together the officer talked about his job, and after being impressed with Terrance's street knowledge, suggested that he apply for the job. The parole officer told Terrance that he thought he could do a lot for the community and the people on parole. He further went on to explain to Terrance that he thought parole was the job he had been looking for, because P.O.'s had a great deal of power over the people that they supervised. If used properly, he told Terrance, this power could effect changes in human behavior. Terrance thanked him for the information, but in the back of his mind he saw parole officer's as cops since they had the power to arrest. The abuse he received from those southern cops left a bad taste in his mouth that he hadn't forgotten.

They didn't help or protect the black communty in his eyes. They were the enemy. He didn't want to be seen that way. Terrance's wife eventually got pregnant and he began to look for ways to make more money because he now had a family to support. One of the draw backs of social work jobs was that the salaries were low. Although Terrance, felt he was effective at times he was frustrated because so many people he attempted to help were slipping through the cracks and dying from either overdoses, violent confrontations, or a new disease called "Aids". He finally came to the conclusion or rationalization that if he was going to be frustrated in his dealings with irrational people, he might as well get paid for it. Consequently, he pulled the business card of the parole officer from his roledex, called him, and inquired about applying for a job as a parole officer. The salaries of officers was twice that of his current salary. He still had some misgivings about taking the job, but when he looked at his baby daughter he knew that he had to do it for her.

Terrance was accepted by New York State Parole as a candidate. He found the training to be interesting and challenging at the same time. Within the first two days of the training several people in the recruit class dropped out realizing that this job was not for them. Terrance wasn't sure either, but he was going to give it a try. He never knew, as did most of the general public what a Parole Officer did. During the training his class was told that while performing their duties they might be called patrol officers, probation officers (a different organization), police officers or any number of other names because sometimes the people who you come in contact with will not know exactly what to call them. He never envisioned himself carrying a gun. He remembered how his college roomates wanted him to buy and carry a gun, and how he had resisted their advice, but this was part of the job, a good paying job. He saw during the training, the dangerous places he might have to go and the dangerous people he might come in contact with. He realized that his social work skills couldn't be his only protection. Until this point in his life Terrance felt that he could go into just about any community, especially black communities, because of the way he carried himself, and be safe. He realized during the training that up until now, once again he had just been lucky. His naïve attitude was changing. Until now Terrance thought that most communities saw him as a helpful healer. He realized during his parole training that those same people probably would now see him as an interfering interloper. Even with this new insight he was still determined to go where the help was needed. Most of the parole training was geared towards the law enforcement and legal aspects of the job. This satisfied most of the recruits as that was why they were there. Terrance didn't challenge these directions because he was the new kid on the block, but in his mind he still wanted to use this job as a way of helping misguided individuals. He didn't know it at the time but his later experiences would come in conflict with his present beliefs.

Terrance's graduation from the parole academy came at a tense time. Organized drug street gangs controlled many areas of New York. He in his naïve way of thinking was going to help, so he volunteered to work in the most dangerous community in Queens NY. When he went to the Central Parole Office to receive his assignment, he was greeted by the Regional Director who sat behind a big desk smoking a big Cuban cigar. The director had salt and pepper wavy hair and a grey handle bar mustache. He looked like he had just vacationed in Florida or the Caribbean as he was tanned. He was surrounded by several other administrators, who looked as if he told them to jump they would say how high. He appeared to be arrogant, and was a bit intimidating. He asked Terrance and the two other rookie officers who volunteered to work Queens a few questions. "Are you sure that you guys want to work this dangerous area? Are you aware of what is going on with the drug gangs and how parole officers have been threatened by these gangs?" All three men answered yes. Terrance was not fully aware, but he heard about the problems during training from some of the trainers. Nevertheless he felt that he was prepared to go in there and change the world. This was what he had been waiting for. He however had not thought about how dangerous it would be. He thought more about changing people's lives, and at the same time making enough money so that he could give his wife and daughter everything they needed and wanted. The Director finally said OK, you guys are assigned to the Queens office; just remember the gangs are taking head shots at officers out there because they know you will be wearing bullet proof vests. All three men looked at each other with some apprehension as they left the director's office.

The next day Terrance walked into the Queens Parole Office and met his new Bureau Chief Booker, who filled him and his fellow rookies in on how dangererous things were in Queens. He was impressed with the fact that all three men graduated in the top percentile of their class and wanted to work in Queens. He warned them to be extremely careful and assigned each of them to a unit. He also urged them to connect themselves to an experienced officer in their unit for help in learning the ropes. Unfortunately for Terrance the officers in his unit were at odds with each other. No one was wrong in the way they did the job because things got done, but there were power struggles as it related to ideas. He found one officer bad mouthing another officer or the supervisor and vice versa. He wondered how this would affect them when they had to do the more dangerous parts of the job together. Would everyone watch each other's backs? Fortunately the supervisor of the unit, George Goldbaum, although not perfect had a vast amount of experience and was willing to work closely with him. He'd been stabbed once during the apprehension and custody of a parole violator. He showed Terrance the wound on his left shoulder and said this was his reminder of how dangerous the job can be. He advised Terrance to never let down his guard, and never trust anyone under parole supervision or their families. He told Terrance that he allowed himself to get stabbed because he assumed that a family member of a parolee would not involve herself in the apprehension of her son. Her tirade during the custody was such a distraction that it enabled her son to grab a knife from a kitchen counter and began swinging it at the officers who were there to arrest him. George's only flaw, as Terrance saw it, was his lack of understanding of the black experience. He had no empathy for those who grew up underprivileged. He saw far too many young black men as being the enemy. If the black man drove a nice car he was a drug dealer. If a black man dressed in nice clothes he bought them because of his involvment in illegal activities or he stole them. If a black man had money in his pocket he had to do something illegal to get it. He forgot there was a black middle class. Terrance often wondered what he thought about him, although he never sensed any signs of prejudice. He did have a reputation among some of the black officers of being a racist but he treated Terrance fairly. Because of his mistrust of parolees at times he was a one man army. Terrance witnessed him one time line up twenty parolees in the office on the wall and search each one for weapons by himself. During one of their early talks George suggested to Terrance that he buy himself a backup gun. All parole officers were issued 38 caliber Smith and Wesson 6 shot revolvers. This was the standard weapon for most law enforcement agencies at the time including the New York City Police and the F.B.I. George felt that it was faster to toss the primary weapon and use the secondary firearm, than it was to reload. Terrance wasn't trained that way but it made sense, so he bought a 5 shot Smith and Wesson "detective special" that he could wear on his ankle. Once he purchased the gun he practiced running up and down his block to make sure he was still mobile with a gun strapped to his ankle. He could, so he knew he'd be alright. Although Terrance now had all of this armament he still felt that his best weapon was his mind. He felt that he could talk his way out of most sticky situations, and not have to use deadly physical force as a first resort. During one early incident Terrance went to visit one of his parolees at his home in a project in Queens. Upon entering the complex and locating the elevator he noticed three young men eyeing him from a short distance away. When the elevator opened Terrance entered followed immediately by all three men. There was a moment of hesitation as no one pushed a button for a floor. Because of this hesitation he immediately thought these men were there to do him harm, so he positioned himself in the elevator so that he could get to his pistol quickly. He then pushed the button to the first floor not wanting to be in the elevator any longer than necessary. One of the men then pushed the elevator button to floor number two. When the elevator began to move Terrance slowly pushed back his jacket exposing his pistol while saying,"So what's happening brothers?" Once they observed that Terrance was armed and his apparently willingness to use it, their aggressive body language changed. Terrance exited the elevator with no one following him. He originally wanted to get off the elevator on the 6th floor so he now waited for the elevator to return. When it did, it was empty. Terrance was sure that the men he shared the elevator with planned to rob him had he not been aware of their intentions. A few months later on his visit to the same project he saw one of the same young men who now knew who he was. He greeted Terrance by yelling to Terrance "What's happening PO?" As time passed although always on guard, he worried less about situations such as that because people in that project got to know him, as he developed a reputation for being tough but fair. He didn't know it at the time but this reputation would serve him well later in his career.

Most parole officers are assigned a partner, once they are assigned to a bureau, and Terrance was no exception. The problem with his new partner was that he was an officer that no one else wanted to partner up with. His name was Bernard Simpson. Bernard wasn't a bad officer as he knew how to do the job. He never appeared to be apprehensive or scared. The reason however that most officers didn't want to partner with him was because he was a born again

Christian, who spent more time than anyone else preaching the word of god in the office. He preached to the other officers. He preached to the parolees that he supervised. He preached to the families of the parolees when he went to their homes or spoke to one of them on the phone. The parolee's many times had no choice but to listen to his rants about God. They didn't want to piss him off because he had control over their freedom. However the officers he worked with didn't want to hear it, so many of them stayed away from him as much as they could. Terrance was stuck with him because of his status as a rookie. The first few months on the job Terrance did go into the field with Bernard. He felt it was safer to be in the street with someone who could watch his back, and at the same time show him the ropes. He tolerated the "Holy Roller's" behavior. He tolerated the prayers before going into the field, and the prayers at the end of the day. Over a period of time however this behavior became annoying especially since his feelings about religion were totally incongruous to those of Bernard. He was told by some of the other officers that they were all taking bets on how long he would last working with Bernard. He did let his partner know how he felt about religion without trying to offend him or end up in a debate, but this seemed to make his partner more determined to convert him. Terrance finally went to his supervisor for help and requested a change of partners. Goldbaum did apologize to Terrance for sticking him with Bernard, but explained that he was the only officer available at the time. He further told him that he thought Terrance was ready to go into the field alone if he chose to. He could also join any other team of officers who were available and do his field work with them. This wouldn't work because most the seasoned officers were pretty much operators who wanted to work solo or had partners they were comfortable with so, Terrance had a difficult time finding anyone who wanted to go into the field with him. Terrance promised himself that if he stayed on this job that in the future he would be more helpful to any rookie that followed him. Supervisor Goldbaum did volunteer to go into the field with him at least once a week until he could get him another partner. Finally he told Terrance that he understood how he felt. He said that his concern, as it had been with other officers Bernard had as partners, was that if they got into a firefight, while they were shooting, Bernard would be praying. He thought Bernard saw himself being protected by a higher power and not by a gun. This action could get both he and his partner killed. Once Terrance was given permission to work alone Bernard seemed to back off preaching. He saw that his partner seemed to be avoiding him. He also realized that Terrance was not going to be one of his converts.

CHAPTER 7

"A DANGEROUS JOB"

All N.Y.S. parolees were required to make weekly, biweekly or monthly visits to the parole office in his neighborhood. The frequency of these visits were determined by how well the parolee was adjusting to life on the street. Terrance's first day of office reporting day, he called into his office a known member of the most notorious drug gang in Queens. He was on parole after serving seven years in prison for attempting to kill a member of a rival gang. He was suspected of committing at least 2 other murders by contract, but the cases were dropped because of a lack of evidence. In one of the cases the witness, a female cab driver, was found dead shot in the head in her home. When the parolee was arrested he had in his possession a pistol with a silencer attached. While Terrance was talking to this parolee Goldbuam and two other officers entered Terrance's office, and without saying a word grabbed the subject by the back of his collar and threw him to the floor. One officer pinned him down by placing a knee in his back while another officer handcuffed him. Goldbaum then preceeded to search him, finding a 9 millimeter glock pistol in his waist band. All this happened while Terrance watched in shock. Goldbaum told Terrance once the parolee was secured in custody that they didn't warn him in advance about what they were getting ready to do because they knew the rookie was untested and they didn't want him to panic. Seeing that action take place, within days of him starting the job, made Terrance question what the hell he had gotten himself into. This wasn't social work. This was a police action. Watching the parolee on the floor in handcuffs Terrance had flashbacks of being thrown against a car and handcuffed by those southern cops. He quickly came back to his senses and realized that although this man was black, he was a killer who took the lives of black people so the action taken was justified. He was beginning to realize that there was going to be a time for social work, and a time to put on the law enforcement cap. He thought to himself that trying to counsel an armed felon defintely would not work. For the first time it hit him how difficult it must be to be a black man in law enforcement. Black people with the power to arrest must be able to do the job knowing that at some point they will have to arrest people of their race, while being aware of the history of black oppression by police officers. Terrance hoped that most African American Officers thought as he did and would not allow any unnecessary force to be used in taking people into custody. He wanted to change the lives of some of these black convicts for the better, but at the same time knew that part of his job, and those in similar positions were to protect the community. How could he or would he find a balance he thought.

Two events happened within months of starting the job that really made Terrance question whether being a parole officer until retirement was wise. He received a call at home one Sunday afternoon from Supervisor Goldbaum explaining that he was needed to help return a member of a local drug gang back to state prison. The subject had escaped after being re-arrested on a parole violation. He was apprehended by the N.Y.P.D. and subsequently turned over to state parole whose job it was to return him to an upstate prison. Goldbaum told Terrance to bring all and any weapons that he possessed for protection. Terrance didn't think much about it because all he owned was his two guns. When he reached the precinct in which the parolee was being held, he met several other officers from his office. He immediately noticed that at least four of them pulled shotguns from the trunks of their personal cars. All of the officers entered the precinct where they met with the precinct captain and four police officers. The concern of the captain and Goldbaum was that since this parolee was a high profile drug member some of his people might attempt to free him on the way back to prison. Since the New York Police had no jurisdiction outside of the New York City limits the seven parole officers, including Terrance would be on their own for the rest of the five hour trip back to the state prison. The parole officers consequently were able to get the New York State Police to help in the escort once the officers left the city limits. The parole officers took the prisoner, who was extremely arrogant, in a passive aggressive way, and placed him in one of three state vehicles. Terrance was assigned the task of riding in the back seat of the vehicle with the prisoner while two other officers, one with a shotgun, was in the front seat. The caravan took off with two New York City Police cars in front followed by the car with the prisoner, followed by two state parole cars. As Terrance rode along keeping one eye on the prisoner and the other watching the surrounding area he began to question his decision once again as to why he took this job. He thought to himself. This is not what I expected? Is the money worth risking my life? What would happen to my daughter if she had to grow up without a father? Hell, he thought if he has do this type of work he might as well have joined the police force, then their starting salaries were much less. The prisoner sensed his apprehension and used it to his advantage. "PO Jackson, what is a smooth brother like you doing locking up brothers? You know you are going to get hurt doing this job "Cause the people I deal with don't play! They don't care what color you are. They will kill you without hesitation." One of the officers sitting in the front of the car realizing what the prisoner was trying to do, turned, looked in the back seat, and told him to shut the fuck up. He smiled, looked at the officer, and complied with the instructions. As the sun set the caravan reached the city limits where the city police broke off their escort. The state parole car carrying Goldbaum took the lead as the three state cars proceeded up the New York Thruway. Terrance inquired as to where and when the state police would meet up with them. He now more than ever sensed the danger in what he was doing. It was dark outside now on a Sunday night, and very few cars were on the highway. At times it seemed that the three state cars were the only cars on the road. He didn't want to show fear but he continually kept checking to make sure that his guns were where they were supposed to be in case he needed them. Touching them gave him confidence. He remembered the feeling of being shot when he was in college and never expected to be placed in that position again, but here he was riding in a car, with a dangerous felon whose boys might want to free him, and were willing to kill to achieve that goal. Two hours into the trip the state car carrying Terrance and the prisoner began to over heat and smoke. The caravan consequently pulled over in pitch darkness to check the damage. The only lights available were those coming from the cars headlights, and the officer's flashlights. The state police escort had not made contact yet, so Goldbaum attempted to contact them on his police radio with no success. A few cars passed by only slowing down enough to see what was going on. As the officers were trying to decide whether they should leave the disabled car and proceed in two vehicles, two dark colored cars with tinted windows pulled over about fifty yards behind the caravan. This suspicious behavior made them react quickly with a decision. The prisoner turned and looked through the rear window after hearing the officer's conversation. He then said "All of youse are in the shit now! My boys are here!" Terrance grabbed the prisoner by the sleeve of his jacket and began to pull him out of the state car, but before doing so he told him, "I might die tonight, but you won't see it because I plan to put a bullet in your head before I go!" Terrance's fear faded at that moment, replaced by anger and rage. He quickly walked to one of the other parole vehicles while pressing his gun to the subject's back, when he observed three cars coming in their direction with lights flashing. Everyone knew it was the State Police escort coming to the rescue. Terrance had never been so happy to see the cops. He turned to the prisoner and said in a soft voice "Guess you ain't escaping tonight!" Seeing the quickly approaching police cars the two dark colored vehicles peeled off wheels screeching as they passed the caravan at break neck speed. The three officers, carrying shot guns pointed them at the vehicles as they passed but didn't fire. It was this incident that taught Terrance that he could overcome his fear if he was angry enough. He knew that he now would have to use this emotion if he was going to stay on this job. A few days later the seven officers met to process what they did right, and what they could have done better. Terrance learned during that meeting that there were people in the agency that were suspected of working for the enemy, which was how they knew that the prisoner was being transported to a state prison on a Sunday night. They were even suspected of sabotaging the state car. He was informed that there were internal investigations going on related to this matter. He was also told by the officers in the meeting, who was suspected of being traitors. Goldbaum told Terrance not to tell these people "Shit" about what he did in his day to day life. Anything he did that was routine could be a problem including the route he used to drive home. He further suggested that he change the route he used to drive home everyday. Never go home the same way two days in a row, he told his rookie parole officer. He also informed Terrance that the files he had on each officer in his unit, containing their home addresses, were under lock and key for a reason.

There was one more incident that happened within months of the attempted prisoner break that let Terrance know that he could do the job. One morning while doing a home visit to check on one of his parolees he was confronted upon ringing the door bell to the residence by the parolee's mother, who immediately began to curse him out for coming to her home so early in the morning. Terrance didn't think it was that early as it was after 9am. This was the time of morning when most people were on their way to work, at work, or preparing to go to work, unless they worked the graveyard shifts. This woman fit into none of these categories. He could smell the stale booze and cigarettes on her breath as she continued to yell at him. He tried not to make the woman any angrier then she already appeared to be, but his patience finally wore thin. He then got angry and told the woman that if he had to listen to her bullshit every time he came to her house he would make her son move somewhere else. The mother realized that she had pushed Terrance to his limit, so she backed off and calmed down. Finishing the home visit Terrance was still angry. He hated this feeling because he had seen too many people lose control while under the influence of this emotion, resulting in their making bad decisions. It always took him time to calm down once he got angry. He didn't like that. He thought Billy's uncontrollable anger was partly responsible for his death. Why beat a helpless drug addict senseless before calling the police unless you have some displaced anger.

Terrance got into his car and within minutes he noticed what he thought was another car carrying four black males following him. Someone in the parole office had previously spotted a car matching the description of this car in areas surrounding the office and alerted everyone. To be sure it was the same car Terrance made a left turn at the next corner. When he did the black BMW made the same left turn. He then made a right turn a couple of blocks away followed by the same car. He was still angry from the confrontation he just had with a hung over black woman, so he was consciously ready to make his move. He first used his agency issued police radio to explain the situation and radio his location. He didn't know how long it would take for the police or other parole officers who heard the transmission to get to him, so he thought that it was better to fight from a position favorable to him. Since his car wasn't bullet proof he decided to pulled into a dead end street, and position his car so that no other cars could get pass him. He then jumped out of the vehicle and took cover behind it. As the BMW passed him several shots were fired. Terrance returned fire hitting the car at least twice. Within seconds of this gun fight the police arrived. Some of the police cars chased the BMW. The four men consequently jumped from the vehicle a couple of blocks away, and all but one escaped, running through the back yards and alleys of a neighborhood that was familiar to them. As officers arrived on the scene both police and parole, a few of them approached Terrance after noticing that he was leaning against his car with tears streaming down his face. One of the parole officers asked him if he was alright while examining Terrance's body for injuries. Observing this examination a police captain, who arrived on the scene, walked up to him and explained that sometimes, during encounters such as the one he just experienced, the body goes into shock and the officer may have been injured and not even realize it. Terrance knew this to be true from his own past experience. He told all concerned that he wasn't hurt physically, only emotionally.

He explained that his tears were a way of releasing some of the anger and rage that he was feeling. Crying made him feel better. It became clear to him after this incident that he had now come across another enemy. He had always thought the enemy was the white power structure, and the police who enforce and protect that structure. Protecting this structure could mean sometimes abusing innocent black people. He now saw another enemy who was willing to enslave their communities by selling heroin and cocaine to their own people, and who would rob the innocent and the elderly in the name of their own survival. He thought about the fact that learning to survive in the world of criminal behavior must be a bitch. You have to constantly look over your shoulder for the police or someone who might recognize that you have been or are in the process of committing a crime. You also have to be aware of your competition. It is probably in your best interest to plan escape routes where you reside in case the police or your competitors show up at your door. If you have been committing crimes in a particular neighborhood, usually your own, you will always have a reputation as a thief, burglar, rapist or murderer. Who wants to live like that Terrance thought, but everyday on this job he saw black, white, Asian, and Hispanic people who accepted this as a way of life. Growing up he knew guys who stepped in and out of criminal activity, but the population he was dealing with now were totally committed to criminal lifestyles. It was do or die!

A consequence of Terrance's shooting incident got him the partner that he wanted as the parole agency determined that although Terrance just happened to be in the wrong place at the wrong time he was not the only target. The word had come down from a drug king pin in prison, who was violated by a parole officer, that the agency should be sent a message. The message was to kill a few parole officers.

Terrance was introduced to Sherry Buchwalt a parole officer with several years of experience. She along with some other officers were transferred to the Queens Parole Office to help in this abysmal situation, where drug dealers controlled and terrorized a whole neighborhood. Sherry was an attractive woman in her early thirties who was married with two daughters. Her husband was a cop. She reminded Terrance at times of his college sweet heart Mary, not in appearance but in attitude. She was no nonsense, and had a reputation for not backing away from danger. Terrance liked that because he had seen some female parole officers become invisible when the rough stuff started. She told Terrance that she was angry because the agency transferred her against her wishes, away from the partner she had for years who was also a female. She said that because she was black and her partner was white everyone called them salt and pepper. She further shared that she felt that because her previous partner was also female, this was the agencies way of discouraging female partnership in spite of the impressive record she and her partner had amassed. There were very few female partnerships in Parole at that time. She told Terrance that if she got a dollar for every time she saw a look of bewilderment when she and her partner walked into a precinct, or a jail with a 200 lb. plus man in handcuffs, and in custody, she would be wealthy. The looks they got from male police officers were laughable. Many times these same officers would stand there waiting for the male officers to come thru the door behind them. When no male officer did, they were sometimes speechless. She explained her feelings and attitude to Terrance so he wouldn't take it personal when he saw her do things that he might not agree with or understand. She felt being black and a female in a male dominated world meant she had to constantly prove herself. She admitted that the women in the agency who intentionally avoided doing the most dangerous things didn't help her cause.

It didn't take long for Terrance to see first hand how his new partner operated. During a home visit to a walkup apartment building (no elevator) when the partners reached the second landing at the top of the third floor, stood two men holding a pitbull on a leash. They were blocking the entrance to the fourth floor which was Sherry and Terrance's destination. Both officers knew that the men were look outs for someone on the third floor. They were challenged by one of the men who said "What you want in this building?" Before Terrance could answer the question Sherry pulled out her gun showed her badge and said "none of your damn business! We ain't here to visit or arrest you so we are coming up the steps!" The pitbull was barking viciously so she ended her comunication with the man holding the dog by saying, "If that dog gets loose I'm going to shoot you before I kill it, now move the hell out of our way!" The men looked at each other and without saying a word decided that they should back away. Terrance was impressed with the skill and fearless attitude she exhibited in dealing with that dangerous situation. At that moment he realized he could learn something from her about how to handle himself in life threatening situations.

There was another incident that happened early in their partnership that was kind of humorous. The neighborhood that the partners covered was basically made up of private homes. Where you find private homes you find pet dogs. In this neighborhood, probably because of all the violence and the excessive amount of burglaries, related to drugs, many people had dogs not only as pets, but also for protection. Parole Officers while in the office had many conversations about their own encounters with mans best friend. Some joked about still having the hair of the dog that bit them. One day upon pulling up to the front of a house during a home visit Terrance told Sherry that she could wait in the car as he was not going into the house, he just wanted to ask the parolee a question. It was parole procedure that both partners should exit their car during home visits to back each other up. This procedure was not always adhered to. Sherry thought that she should follow policy after she saw a huge hairy dog tied up on the side of the house, who didn't appear to be friendly. She even suggested that they come back to the house later. Terrance told her it wasn't necessary because he knew the famly and he could see that the dog was tied up far enough away from the entrance that he could ring the door bell safely. Although she didn't agree with him she let him go. When Terrance reached the front gate of the home he looked at the dog from a distance to double check whether or not the dog was tied up securely. He appeared to be secured with thick rope so, Terrance opened the gate and entered the front yard leaving the gate open as he had been trained to do, just in case he needed to escape quickly. He rang the door bell, all the time keeping an eye on the dog who was strenuously attempting to break free of the rope. Suddenly the rope snapped. Terrance's motor memory immediately took charge, as he reflected back to his childhood days where if chased by one of the local dogs you jumped up on the hood of the nearest car. For some reason none of the dogs in the neighborhood ever followed him or any of his friends up on the hoods of those cars. Car hoods were a safety zone from dogs in his neighborhood. Seeing the rope brake and the dog charge at him Terrance broke out running full speed looking at the hood of the car in which Sherry was sitting. To her credit her quick thinking saved Terrance from being bitten. Realizing that she couldn't reach across to open the passenger side door quickly she decided to roll down the electric passenger side front window. Although Terrance was initially heading for the hood of the car he now focused in on the open window diving head first through the window into the car just as the dog was snapping at his heels and rear end. Sherry quickly rolled up the window then turned to him and said loudly "Dumb ass! I told you so!" After Terrance's heart stopped beating a million miles a minute, and realizing that he was alright, they looked at each other and started laughing. Terrance told her he knew that she wasn't going to let him live this one down. There was a lesson learned by Terrance from this incident, "Action was quicker than reaction" as the dog was on top of him so fast that he didn't have time to pull his weapon. He heard that phrase before during training and now he experienced what it meant. From then on whenever he was going into a situation that he perceived as dangerous he would put his weapon, in his hand, in his pocket, that way he was always ready to react quickly.

CHAPTER 8

"COP OR SOCIAL WORKER"

Terrance was able to use his social work skills, which had always been his main reason for joining the agency. He used the tremendous amount of power that parole officers in New York State had to push men and women under his supervision to make the tough decisions about their lives. The threat of reincarceration was a powerful and persuasive tool. He tried never to abuse his power, but came close many times in trying to achieve an objective. He justified his behavior with the thought that he was doing what was in the best interest of the parolee, because he cared. So at times he felt bad about what he did. More than once he forced mothers who were under his supervision, and who had minor children to care for, into residential treatment programs. He hated to separate children from their mothers, but he understood those women would be no good to their children until they could first take care of themselves. On another occasion he violated a parolee because along with some other charges he dropped out of a school where he was learning to read and write (he might have overlooked the other charges if the man had stayed in school). Terrance was sure that he was doing the right thing as many of these people had poor or no support systems and even less self control. He began to think that jail, unfortunately, was the only answer for some. If they were left on the street without structure he knew they would commit more crimes, it wasn't rocket science. He once had a discussion with one of his parolee's where he urged him to hang out with his more positive friends. The parolee responded by saying that he had no positive friends or relatives. He went on further and explained that his father and all of his uncles were either in prison or been in prison. He also had one brother who just came home from jail and one still there. When asked if the prison experience changed any of them for the better. He responded "Mr J old habits die hard." Terrance knew that he was doing some things right when he would occasionally get a call from a parent or wife telling him to please continue to do what ever he was doing with the parolee because it was working. One time while lodging a parolee, that he had arrested, in a local jail, the correction officer overheard the parolee thank Terrance as he was taking off the handcuffs. The correction officer responded to what he heard by asking the parolee "What the hell is wrong with you? This man is locking you up and you are thanking him!" The parolee answered the officer by explaining that Officer Jackson had treated him more than fairly and that his arrest this time was totally his own fault.

Sherry admitted during some of their discussions that Terrance's attitude about trying to save some of the people they supervised had been lost by her because of all the attention she had placed on dealing with the "scum bags." She described a scum bag as someone who chose to continue a criminal lifestyle when they had other options. She said that sometimes on the job you forget that not everybody on parole is a totally bad person. Sometimes they are just people who made bad decisions. Terrance told her that he believed that sometimes mistakes could be forgiven and corrected and that he never wanted to lose sight of that. He spent hours, when he could, talking to parolee's. He wanted to understand the criminal mind. He also determined that even in the criminal world people specialized. Crimes such as burglary, bank robbery, or car theft are specialties. He talked to car thieves about how they stole cars, what type of tools they used, and what if anything would discourage them from stealing a car. He talked to burglars about how they chose a house. What was the best time of the day or night to commit the burglary? He asked men and women convicted of murder what they thought pushed them to take a life.

Around this time Terrance was assigned a parolee of Italian decent, whose brother was the head of a New York organized crime family. This man had a long affliation with his brother's crime family and this fascinated Terrance. He watched a lot of gangster movies when he was growing up. Whenever Terrance had the time the two of them would talk about the mafia or organizations, such as that. Pauly "Jughead" Sornese would never give his parole officer any direct information about the inner workings of his organization, which he denied existed, but he liked him so he would entertain him with alleged fictional tales. Pauly was a five foot one, stocky, balding, Italian man with flat feet that appeared to bother him when he walked. If not for the fact that his brother was a mafia kingpin he probably would have gotten his ass kicked every day in prison. However no one messed with him because the people who did turned up missing. He was pleasant and cooperative as was everyone on parole assigned to Terrance's caseload with organized crime connections. He was paroled after serving 5 years in prison for enterprise corruption. He and his crew imported heroin into the country from Columbia and distributed it on the streets of New York, and New Jersey, to their dealers. Pauly also owned an auto glass repair shop which he listed as his source of income. Although he couldn't prove it, Terrance was sure that this business was a front for laundering drug money. Pauly was married with two children. His wife was a well paid Wall Street stock broker. He listed his sources of income as profits from his auto glass business and, his wife's salary. His business was suspected on a couple of occasions of breaking out the window glass of cars for several blocks in the neighborhood so that their owners would have to get them repaired. Pauly's business always benefited from this rash of smashed windows. Whenever Terrance visited Pauly's modest home in an expensive neighborhood, Pauly would offer him an espresso to drink while they talked. Terrance loved espresso. During some of these talks Terrance would sometimes try and catch him off guard with a direct question about someone in his brother's mob. Pauly would respond" Mr J if I tell you I got to kill you." He would then look at Terrance and smile. If there was such a thing as a good guy, bad guy bond the two men developed one.

A year after Terrance was assigned Pauly's case he became eligible for an early release from parole. Pauly had been under parole supervision for over three years including the time spent with his present PO. Terrance was given permission to conduct an investigation which could lead to Pauly's discharge from parole if the report was approved by the Board of Parole. Everyone in the agency knew that Pauly was still involved with illegal activity with his brother, but no one could prove it, including Terrance. There were times when Pauly would indirectly challenge Terrance to prove he was doing something wrong. He once told Terrance "I am a criminal. My job is to do things that are illegal. Your job is to try and catch me." Terrance with Sherry's help, and that of other agencies including the FBI, could not connect him to anything illegal. Terrance actually admired the artful craftiness Pauly exihibited. Pauly knew he was being watched by several different law enforcement agencies but he didn't care. He didn't think any of them were good enough to catch him again. He learned from his last conviction what not to do, so as not to get caught. During another of their conversations he told his PO that once in a while he would have fun. Once he identified the car that was following him on a particular day, he would walk up to the car and tell the men inside where he was going next, just in case they lost sight of him. He said that on another occasion he purposely evaded being followed only to park and watch them ride around looking for his car like the Keystone Cops of silent films.

Terrance conducted his investigation using all of the tools at his disposal. He was unable to find a reason to reject Pauly's parole discharge. He knew he was dirty but couldn't prove it. He knew that "it's not what you know, it's what you can prove." He didn't feel bad because neither could the FBI, the DEA, or the NYPD. Consequently his report recommended that Mr Sornese be discharged from parole. A few months after submitting the report Terrance received a notice from the Parole Board that Pauly's request to be discharged was rejected. When Pauly was given the news, he asked Terrance what he could do to challenge the Parole Board's decision. Terrance explained that since the board members were appointed by the Governor the buck stopped with them, unless he knew someone in the Governor's office. His other alternative was to get a lawyer and challenge the outcome of the report. He then asked Terrance if he could recommend an attorney. It just so happened that he did. Terrance didn't think anything was wrong with turning Pauly onto a lawyer who could help him. He knew the reason his discharge was turned down was purely political. He had seen others with less impressive reports receive discharges.

Jake Sullivan was a fearsome lawyer who fought to defend the rights of people who were violated by parole. He was a sloppy dressing man, that many people who were involved in the parole violation process made fun of because of the way he dressed and carried himself. Many times he appeared in court wearing clothes he appeared to have slept in. His suits were wrinkled and the white shirts he wore, usually had dirty collars and dirty sleeves. He was the cartoon character Charlie Brown's "Pig Pen" squared. Terrance was able look beyond how he was dressed, although he did laugh with others at him on occasion. He admired how Jake pressed issues in court in defense of the parolees that he defended, in spite sometimes, of overwhelming evidence against them. They could get caught with a gun in their pockets or drugs hidden in their socks. It didn't matter, Jake would try and use some legal maneuver to get the case dismissed or the parolee found not guilty. He was well versed on parole law so Terrance thought he might be the person to help the parolee. He gave Pauly Jake's business card after getting Jake's approval.

A week later Terrance received a call from Jake. "What the hell did you get me into?" Jake screamed into the phone. Terrance wanted to know what he was talking about, and why he was so angry. Jake told him that he and Pauly decided to meet for the first time in a local diner. He continued to explain that he took some notes and received a check from Pauly as a retainer. After leaving the diner he went to visit a friend in Forest Hills, the home at one time of the US Open Tennis Tournament. Jake said that when he left his friends apartment he found that someone had broken into his car, and his briefcase which housed the notes from his meeting with Pauly were taken from the trunk. He reported the break in to police. The next morning he received a call from the police telling him that they found his brief case and that he could come and retreive it. When he retrieved his property all of his paperwork was still in the briefcase. During the car breakin he thought it was strange that nothing else was taken from his car. Terrance told him how Pauly on many occasions was followed by law enforcement agencies who were trying to make cases against him. The two of them after talking, figured that someone followed Pauly to the diner and after they left the diner followed Jake, subsequently breaking in his car and taking his briefcase.

Since both men figured that criminals would not have turned the briefcase in to the police it had to be someone in law enforcement. Jake figured that someone probably made photo copies of the papers and returned everything back to him. He never got a satisfactory explanation from the police concerning how his briefcase was found.

Within a year with Jake's legal help Pauly was discharged from parole. Upon receiving notice that he was discharged Pauly called Terrance on the phone to thank him for his help. He told Terrance that he thought he was an honorable man because he had the power to block his discharge but he didn't in spite of the way he felt. He said that if there was ever anything that he could do to repay him, he only had to ask. Terrance responded by saying, "Dumb ass, did you ever consider that your phone is being tapped, and probably so is this conversation; so thanks but no thanks, good luck and stay out of trouble." Terrance then hung up the phone, leaned forward on his desk, shook his head and laughed. He later thought about the fact that he called a "made man" a dumb ass. He let his mouth, because he was angry, in that moment, cash a check that he couldn't cover. Terrance didn't realize how grateful Italian mobsters could be. Pauly was extremely grateful so he was willing to overlook things Terrance might say, that he would kill someone else for saying. He also received a call from Jake who thanked him for the referral. He told Terrance that not only did he get paid a handsome fee but he got some refferals from Pauly. He was warned by Terrance to be careful. He reminded him that although Pauly appeared to be a nice guy he could be dangerous if you got too close. "Money ain't everything" he told Jake. He then shared a story that Pauly shared with him during one of their talks. Apparently Pauly's older brother was a heavy heroin user. The best dope in town was dealt by the South Jamaica Queens Gang, so he did business with them on a regular basis. On one of his trips to buy drugs he was robbed and beat up subsequently dying from his injuries a few days later. The cops knew who did it, but didn't have enough evidence to arrest the perpetrators of the crime. By the time they gathered enough information to make an arrest the two black men were found in a swamp area by Kennedy Airport shot in the head execution style. Without admitting he knew anything about the demise of the men he shared with Terrance that his family wanted their mothers to cry like his mother did when his brother died.

CHAPTER 9

"ONE RUTHLESS GANG"

Unlike the Italian mobs who basically only did harm to rival criminals, the black drug gangs in South Jamaica, Queens, would harm anyone that they thought was a threat to their business. Grandmoms, ministers, and children were not off limits. Their ruthless behavior saddened Terrance because he had always been about black unity not black destruction. He equated their attitudes and behavior to that of some African Nations where one tribe brutally raped and murdered the members of another tribe, in the name of ethnic or religious cleansing. However this was not about anything other than the control of drugs in their neighborhood for profit.

South Jamaica Queens, New York during this time period, was not what one would call the ghetto. It was made up mostly of hard working blue collar and professional people. They owned homes. They went to church and they tried to raise their children to be responsible. Unfortunately many of their children became victims of the drug trade that targeted their community. This community was a perfect example of what illegal drugs could do to destroy an African American neighborhood. Terrance and Sherry along, with most of the other parole officers in their office found themselves spending most of their time dealing with the effect of heroin and cocaine. They would have much rather perferred helping improve the lives of the people under their supervision. But then many of those same people might not be involved with the criminal justice system if not for drugs.

During dangerous times most law enforcement partnerships become closer than ever. Sherry and Terrance's partnership was no exception. Their families began to spend time together when not working, and when they were working the street they worked extremely well together, as they watched each other's backs.

The second in command of the notorious neighborhood drug gang the Green Knights, was assigned to Sherry caseload. The gang chose the name because their leadership board sat around a round table such as did King Arthur and his Knights to discuss business on how to control the drug trade which made them money which is green in color.

Ronald "Champion" Duncan, was a 35 year old black man who had a criminal history dating back to the age of 10. He was a man with no distinctive marks or tatoos. He dressed down not wearing stylish clothes or expensive jewelry. He usually came to the office wearing worn jeans and bo-bo sneakers. When spoken to, he responded in a soft non threating voice. You never would imagine that this man from his demeanor had a criminal history which included drug sales, rape, grand larceny, and attempted murder. He was also in charge of a multi million dollar drug empire. He had been able to avoid serious jail time because his attorneys were able to convince the court system that he had a low IQ level. To Terrance this meant that although he was intelligent enough to oversee a drug empire because of his low IQ he should not be punished for his crimes. Terrance wasn't buying this bullshit. If you did the crime you should do the time. Terrance saw this man as a quiet ticking time bomb. When he looked at you it was if he was staring right through you with his cold light brown eyes. Out of all the people he had been in contact with since becoming a parole officer, he felt that Duncan was by far the most dangerous. When examining prison records Sherry read that Champion had been running the drug empire from jail, along with the top man who was serving life for murdering his wife. Terrence warned his partner that they should be very careful about how they handled this guy. She wasn't buying his warning. She was not going to treat him any different than any other parolee. She wasn't scared or intimidated by him. Terrance wasn't either, but he felt this man was not just another hub cap stealing crackhead. The partners decided to develop their own organizational chart of the drug gang in the neighborhood they covered as many of them were being released from prison and assigned to parole. During their investigation they also found that besides being a drug captain Ronald Duncan also was the gang's negotiator. When there was a dispute between his gang and another gang over territory he would work out their differences avoiding bloodshed. This was definitely a position of power. What complicated the supervision of these parolees also was the fact that there were parole staff who were suspected of feeding them information on how to avoid problems with parole. These people were also suspected of giving the drug gang information on the members of rival drug gangs such as their home adddresses, and people on parole they thought were snitches. Terrance and Sherry decided that the information that they put together was only going to be shared with a select few.

Around this time supervisor Goldbaum was promoted. He was replaced by a man who eventually would be one of Terrance's best friends in the agency besides being his mentor. Carlos Rodriguez had a reputation of being a parole officer's supervising parole officer. He backed his officers to the hilt. Coincidently he and Goldbaum had been partners when they worked the street. He was organized and spoke Spanish fluently. He understood the complexities involved in dealing with parolees but at times he would rather lock up someone than help them work through their problems and keep them on the street. He was Terrance's alter ego. This became an issue of contention between the two early in their relationship. Terrance taught him to soften his position when appropriate and he taught Terrance how to be tough when it was necessary. He and Terrance spent hours arguing about whether or not to lock up someone for minor offenses. Carlos felt that it was much easier to lock up a parolee for violating the rules than to spend time trying to change his or her behavior. He was old school in his thinking as many of the older officers opted for incarceration over behavior modification. Terrance was among the new breed of officers, who wanted to use arrest as a last resort rather than the first option. What Terrance admired most about Carlos was that they would disagree about how to handle a case to the point of sometimes yelling at each other, but he never took it personal. When they finished yelling and screaming at each other about the merits of a case he would say to Terrance "now that this has been settled, let's go out after work and get a drink," which the men did many times. Terrance knew of other supervisors who would take his different thought process as a direct challenge to their authority and use this challenge to punish his subordinate officers. Carlos was confident enough not to think that way. One time during a meeting before their unit went out to execute a warrant, the group discussed going into a Muslim Mosque to arrest someone they were sure was there seeking asylum. Terrance told the group that he was not about to go into a holy place with guns drawn to make an arrest. He pointed out to the group that they would not consider doing this in a Catholic or Protestant church. The group backed off and agreed that he was right. Carlos then asked him would he be willing to go into the Mosque and speak to the Iman. He agreed to do so. When the team arrived at the Mosque Terrance received permission to enter, and after removing his shoes he was led into the office of the Iman, where he explained the situation. To his surprise the Iman surrendered the parolee without incident. When he walked out of the mosque with the parole violator in handcuffs he saw the admiring looks on the faces of his fellow officers, including Carlos, who later admitted that if not for Terrance's intervention he would have handled the arrest differently. He also said that his way would probably have caused problems. Terrance pointed out to him that everyone in the community was not a criminal and therefore were reasonable people, who also had the protection of their neighborhood at heart. Every person of color was not the enemy.

Terrance heard stories about some of the older parole officers, mostly white men, who would force their way into the homes of African Americans, with guns drawn looking for parole violators, while there were small children running around the house. Sometimes elderly people would also be exposed to this behavior. These officers weren't trained that way but their lack of respect for the law abiding black people in the community enabled them to justify their abuse of power. Terrance was determined to not be that type of officer. He chose that viewpoint, and as a result was sometimes perceived as being soft on his parolees. He didn't care, because he felt he was doing the right thing. Hell he thought how could I be soft? I shot back at men who were trying to kill me, just because I was a parole officer. Most of the officers who thought him soft had never had that experience, so what did they know. Terrance believed that if you treated someone like a criminal that was the way they would relate to you. However if you treat them with respect, where possible, you in most cases would get respect in return. When people respect you they will usually listen to what you have to say, even if they don't agree with you. If you can get a parolee to listen to what you have to say, then that's a barrier broken down. Even when making arrests Terrance was always cognizant of how he treated his prisoners. He wasn't truly altruistic. When possible it also was a smart way to avoid resistance during an arrest. This mutual respect also helped him better control sticky situations. He wished that he had gotten that type of respect from some of his fellow white officers when he first started the job.

A new breed of officer joined the parole ranks at the same time as Terrance. Many of the officers, black, white, and female, thought the way he did. Many of the new officers, mainly black and Hispanic, were constantly challenged by white officers when they entered some of the parole offices. To some of these officers all people of color walking into the office were on parole. One day Terrance entered a Manhattan Parole office, after leaving court, at the request of his supervisor to deliver some paperwork before returning to Queens. He was dressed in a three piece suit and upon getting off of the elevator leading to the office area, he was confronted by four white officers who asked him what he was doing in the parole officer area. Without allowing him to answer they told him to get out and enter the building through the door designated for parolee's and the general public. Terrance waited a minute to allow his anger to subside before speaking. He flashed back to his time in Florida dealing with racism and thought to his self "I know how to handle these guys." He took a couple of deep breaths and asked them if he could show them some ID before reaching into his pocket. One of the officers answered "yes, but you better not bring anything else out of your pocket," as he placed his hand on the 38 pistol he had on his waist. Terrance didn't verbalize in advance that he was a parole officer so when he pulled a gold shield like theirs from his pocket all four men backed up astonished and embarrassed, but not embarrassed enough to apologize. They all just walked away without saying another word. Other black and Hispanic officers would later share similar experiences with him.

On another occasion Terrance went with three old timer parole officers to arrest one man. When the officers entered the apartment which was on the third floor the subject barricaded himself in his bedroom. When they broke down the door and entered the room the parolee backed himself into a corner by a window and threatened them with a knife he held in his hands. He was swinging the knife back and forward while frantically yelling "Come and get me mother fuckers!" All of the officers pulled their guns and were prepared to shoot him, all of the officers except Terrance. From his view of the situation he thought there might be another way to resolve this Mexican standoff which was obvious to him that the parolee would lose. He quickly pushed his way past his fellow officers and asked them to hold their fire. He positioned himself off to the side between the parolee and the parole officers. He didn't want to get in the line of fire in case someone got trigger happy, and he didn't want to get too close to the parolee in case he decided to attack. He remembered that while in the recruit class he had seen how quickly someone with a knife could attack before someone with a holstered gun could pull it and fire, if they were close enough. He then turned to the parolee and said, "What the hell are you doing? Do you want to die, because if this is your goal there are three men standing on the other side of this room who are ready and willing to help you achieve it! Take a good look around the room," Terrance urged him to do. "There is no way out of here unless you want to jump out the window. What are you on parole for," Terrance asked him? He replied that he was convicted of selling a couple pounds of marajuana to an undercover police officer, and he had not reported to the parole office as required, over the past 2 months. Terrance then responded, "So you are willing to die for the minor offense of failing to report? Does that make sense?" Terrance now watched the parolee's body language begin to change as he slowly lowered the knife while thinking about Terrance's questions. He took advantage of what he saw by suggesting to the man with the knife that he probably wouldn't do a lot of jail time on this minor offense. He further suggested that he would probably be back on the street before he knew it. From another room in the apartment everyone heard the subject's wife yell "Phil please listen to him!" Hearing his wife plead with him the parolee looked down at the floor and dropped the knife. Two of the officers moved in quickly and handcuffed him. As they were leaving the apartment the parolee's wife thanked Terrance for his intervention. One of his fellow officers looked back at them and said "Yeah she should thank you because I was prepared to tear him a new asshole if he didn't drop the knife."

Sherry was a headstrong female, so after a period of time supervising Ronald Duncan she wanted to follow him for a period of time because she suspected he was back to his old tricks. The partners had used this tactic spending many hours and gallons of gas following Pauly Sornese only to come up empty. Terrance followed his partners lead as they began surveillance on Mr Duncan. One time they even thought they were made by him. Terrance wanted to break off the surveillance but Sherry said "No." She wanted to follow him anyway just to see what he did. Sherry did take her partner's advice in some instances, as every time Ronald visited the office, before they talked, she would search him for weapons, just to be on the safe side. The word on the street was that he was carrying a gun.she was hoping to find a gun. Champion was too smart to get caught that easy. One time though, Ronald called the office on a day when he was supposed to report to say that he didn't feel well because the gun shot wound he received years before was bothering him, to the point where he had trouble walking. He asked to be excused from reporting. Sherry excused him and told him to just report the next week. Later in the day she got word that he was seen on the street, so she and Terrance got into their state car and drove to the area where he was reported being seen. A half a block away they parked and watched Champion Duncan standing on a corner with several other men. He was holding a forty ounce bottle of beer while dancing to the music which was playing on a boom box. Terrance wanted Sherry to drive up and arrest him for lying to her, and for drinking beer in public, but she smiled and ruled that idea out. She told him that what the parolee was doing would only end up in a Mickey Mouse arrest which would only send him back to prison on a parole violation for a short period of time. Besides there were several other men on that corner and she wasn't sure what weapons they might have on them. She didn't want to call for police backup to arrest someone for dancing on the street with a forty ounce bottle of beer in his hand. Sherry wanted to catch him doing something serious so he would go back to jail for a long time. She felt that if she was patient she would achieve that goal.

It wasn't long before Sherry got her wish. So much pressure was put on Ronald Duncan by law enforcement agencies, including Parole, that he cracked under the pressure. Within a two day period of time he was accused of raping a 15 year old girl at gun point, and also fit the description of a man who raped a 17 year old boy. The icing on the cake happened when a known drug dealer from the Bronx was found shot in the head execution style, after his car was set on fire in a swamp area of Northern Jersey. Among the things recovered from the scene of the car fire was paperwork identifying Mr Duncan as someone under New York State Parole supervision. Based on all of this information Sherry was able to get a warrant for his arrest. Parole Officers in New York always tried to maintain good working relationship, with the NYPD. They did many times, however, believe that they were being used. They were left out of the loop on occasions when they shouldn't have been. They were only called when a cop needed some help on a case, and they many times took parolees into custody and held them for the police with no thanks for their efforts not even from their own agency. In spite of this situation many officers tried to develop a personal relationship with one or two cops in case they needed them. Terrance and Sherry were no different. They developed a professional relationship with a salt and pepper team of cops named Ollie and Jimmy. These officers rode together everyday and worked the same precinct as Terrance and Sherry. They backed the parole officers up when they were making arrests on many occasions. The partners both lived in Long Island, Ollie in Hempstead and Jimmy in Levittown. They had been working together for 7 years and as a result became very close. Ollie was the more aggressive member of the team. Terrance always thought that Ollie being African American felt he had to prove himself to his fellow police officers, who were mostly white. Terrance never witnessed him do anything dirty to anyone he arrested, but he always seemed to use just a little more force than some situations called for. Jimmy was more laid back and seemed to be comfortable being the only white member of the four officers. The police, parole and the FBI were all now looking for Champion Duncan. The FBI was called in on the case because it was believed that the drug dealer was killed in New York and then driven to New Jersey where his car was set on fire making it an interstate case. The FBI was also aware of Champion's past criminal involvement with an organized drug gang with international ties.

When it came to cases of this magnitude it was every agency for themselves. Everyone wanted credit for this apprehension and arrest. No one was sharing information, not at least through above board channels. Sherry wanted to apprehend Duncan in the worst way. Capturing him, she felt, would put a big feather in her cap within the agency. Terrance tried many times to convince her that she had a stellar reputation on the job. She still wasn't satisfied. At first she was not given the approval to recruit enough parole officers to work the case the way she wanted. The best and worst thing that could have happened was that Champion became implicated in the murder of a drug dealer, in another state. The agency at first didn't want to approve the overtime on the rapes as they wanted the work to be done by the New York City Police Department, subsequently saving money on overtime. When the crimes that he was accused of committing escalated to murder for the second time, they thought it in their best interest politically to approve the time necessary to find and arrest this criminal. Terrance learned early in his parole career that the NYS Division of Parole was a political agency, and that politics sometimes dictated the decisions that were made. He later found out that the police were also hoping that parole would use their resources to make the arrest based on the initial crimes of rape, using the same philosophy of saving money on overtime. It was not that these agencies were not making an effort to apprehend Champion. He just was not a political priority. Everybody was trying to save money, so what if a 15 year old black girl was forced into a car at gun point and raped after her 16 year old boyfriend was pistol whipped. The second murder implication seemed to raise the bar motivating parole to invest more man power in making an arrest.

Sherry put together a team of 10 officers from three different parole units to work the case around the clock. Ollie and Jimmy, although working with their fellow police officers on the case, agreed to back channel information they gathered to Sherry and she would do the same to them. The officers working the case followed up on tips they received. They staked out places he was known to frequent. During their investigation Terrance and Sherry tracked him to an apartment of an old girlfriend in Brooklyn without any success in finding him. His old girlfriend told them that he had been in her apartment but she wouldn't let him stay because she knew he was on the run and she didn't want to expose her children to danger. The ex girlfriend further told them that she had always been turned on by men who lived on the edge. She loved bad boys, admitting that the father of her two children was doing time for bank robbery. She said that her baby's father got caught after he volunteered to be in a police line up to make $25.00. He didn't know it at the time, nor did he ask, but the line up was set up because the police and FBI had a suspect in three bank robberies. Unfortuately for him all three bank tellers identified him in the line up as one of the stick up men, not the suspect who was in custody. The police then took him into custody seizing his cellphone along with the rest of his property. When they checked the numbers on his phone they found that he had called all three banks just days before the robberies. What a stupid bad boy! Crime solved, go directly to jail! Since Sherry and Terrance were sure that he had been in the area they put a wanted flyer under every door of the 200 apartments in that project complex. They searched Champions apartment numerous times looking for leads as to his whereabouts. They traveled as far south as Washington DC on a tip that he might have fled there. A few weeks passed and no one seemed to know where Champion was hiding. New York City Police put undercover police officers in every city prison hoping someone would talk. The FBI bugged the residences of people he was known to associate with but had no luck. Sherry wasn't discouraged. She thought that she had the inside track on finding him as she previously made a good connection with his sister, who was a New York City Corrections Officer. His sister hated what her brother had done to the community where she lived. She felt that he represented the worst in black men. She pointed out to Sherry that they were raised in the same house, yet her brother chose to be a criminal. She believed that anyone who had options in life and chose to be a criminal was mentally ill. For that reason she agreed with a court evaluation that her brother had a low IQ which played a part in his criminal behavior. Terrance and Sherry both agreed with her assessment that her brother had mental health issues but they felt that it had nothing to do with his IQ. They thought that he was just a sociopath.

While Sherry was obsessed with capturing Champion, Terrance was cautious. He was sure that this guy was not going to go quietly. He knew that any mistakes made in any action that they took could be fatal. Because they were now looking to arrest a person more dangerous than the average parolee that they came into contact with on a daily basis, this lead to more interactions with some of the most dangerous people walking the streets of New York. It became clear to him during this period of time that if the general public was aware of how many dangerous people were walking the streets, they would be up in arms. Fortunately for the public, since you can't keep all the bads guys locked up forever, parole agencies were effective in helping to protect them, while keeping a low community profile. On one occasion during this period someone told Sherry that Champion was just seen sitting in a van outside the parole office with three other men, while waiting for someone who just came into the office. The parolee who was driving the van was questioned in the office. He denied Champion being outside in his vehicle. Sherry, and neither did anyone else believe him because of his prior association to this sociopath. She then started out of the building alone with her hand on her gun, when Terrance jumped in front of her and stopped her. "Are you crazy? What the hell are you doing?" Terrance yelled! She responded that she was not going to approach the van alone. She just wanted to see if she could spot Champion sitting in the car. It made her angry to think that her prey had the balls to sit in a vehicle right outside of the parole office knowing that he is a wanted man. By the time they walked back to their office the supervisor had recruited several officers to approach the van and search it. "Sherry, where the hell did you go?" He yelled! We were looking for you! Sherry quickly responded "Ah, I had to go to the ladies room." Terrance following her into the room and hearing her response just looked up at the ceiling and noded his head in disbelief. The parole officers left the building in three teams of three. They all approached the van from different directions and on the signal from the supervisor rushed up, opened the doors and pulled all four occupants out making them all lay face down on the ground. Champion was not in the van. One of the men in the van was however taken into custody, after it was determined that he had an open warrant.

There was another time during Sherry's obsession over Champion's capture that she received a tip that he might be hiding out in an apartment in Brooklyn, that she had not been to before. She recruited Terrance and two other parole officers to accompany her. The officers arrived at the twelve story building. Sherry then located and questioned the building landlord. He couldn't identify a photo of Champion as someone he had seen around but he did tell her that the apartment she was looking for was on the tenth floor. The officers took the elevator to the tenth floor where Sherry knocked on the door to the apartment of interest. A man answered through the door "Who is it?" Sherry responded loudly "The police open the door!" There were a couple of minutes of silence as the officers could hear shuffling going on inside the apartment. Sherry knocked on the door again and yelled "Open this door right now!" The door was then opened by a woman with a heavy Caribbean accent. She was dressed scantly in a tight haulter top and daisy duke jeans that were so tight that it didn't appear that she was wearing panties. "Can I help you" she asked?" Sherry explained to the woman that she had a warrant for the arrest of Ronald "Champion Duncan" and asked if she knew him. The woman answered that she did know Champion but that he wasn't in the apartment. Sherry told the woman that she had to search anyway as she pushed the woman aside and entered the apartment followed by the other three parole officers. Upon entering the residence and following parole procedure the woman was told to ask everyone who was in the apartment to come into the living room. She followed these instructions and one by one, four women came into the room from different areas. The women were told to have a seat on the sofa while the officers searched. What was immediately obvious was that no men came into the living area, only women. All the women denied that there were any men in the apartment. Sherry turned to Terrance and asked him if he heard a man's voice when they originally knocked on the door? He and both the other officers answered in the affirmative. "He is here she whispered!" All four officers now pulled their pistols. Sherry, Terrance, and one officer searched while the fourth officer watched the ladies sitting in the living room. The three officers now feeling that someone was hiding in the apartment cautiously worked their way down the long hallway, which had doors on both sides, room by room and closet by closet. When they reached the end of the hall and searched the last room, which was a bathroom, they were puzzled because they found no one. They walked back into the living room while trying to convince themselves that they did a thorough search. They stood in the living room area for a few minutes, talking about the search and the man's voice they initially thought they heard. While they talked one of the women, who was dressed in short tight jeans blurted out "I told you no one else was here!" Still not convinced because there were no fire escape stairs on the outside of the building, and they were on the tenth floor, they decided to search again. Sherry said that she knew Champion was an escape artist, so he had to be in the apartment somewhere. This time when they searched, Terrance stayed in the living room to watch the ladies replacing the other officer. He thought a new pair of eyes might see something that he didn't see. It took the three officers another twenty minutes to search again without any luck. Puzzled and confused about what they thought they previously heard they pondered on the situation and decided that there was nothing else that they could do but leave. Before leaving Terrance happened to look out of the big bay windows in the living room to gaze at the panoramic view of Brooklyn. While quickly gazing out the window he looked down. He then motioned Sherry to come to the window. "Is that him?" he said pointing down at the ground. Sherry placed her hand to her mouth in shock before running out of the apartment followed by the other three officers. When they reached the ground floor they all ran around to the side of the building where they saw the body of a man lying lifeless on the ground. A crowd had already started to gather so they had to push their way through to get a good look at the man. Sherry immediately observed that it was not her prey. "Damn, it's not him" she said with a disappointed look on her face. Paramedics came to the scene along with the police. They pronounced the man lying on the ground, in a pool of blood, dead. It was later ascertained that the man named John La-Pierre was wanted by New York State Parole on a violation. He apparently climbed out on to the window ledge during the search of the apartment. While out there he must have lost his balance falling ten stories to his death.

The next day when Sherry returned to the parole office, she found a large window pane at least 4 feet high sitting on top of her desk. She laughed when she saw it and then yelled out to the staff "Everyone's got jokes."

There was another incident during the search for Champion that Terrance was glad he was part of, for Sherry's sake. Champion had a brother who because he was gay had disassociated himself from the family. Sherry found out from Champion's sister where he lived and took Terrance along to go talk with him. She was assured by Champion's sister that her brother Donald was not in contact with his brother. "Champion hates him simply because he is a homosexual" she said. She thought that the last place he would hide was with his brother just for that reason. Sherry didn't care. She wanted to cover every base no matter how small or insignificant others thought it might be.

The two officers subsequently went to the apartment and knocked on the door. The man answering the door identified himself while talking in a very feminine voice as Donald Duncan. The officers identified themselves and then were allowed into the small but neatly decorated apartment. Upon entering they both heard the shower running in the bathroom. Donald told them that a female friend was in the bathroom using his shower. Donald then answered a series of questions posed to him by the partners. Sherry then said before leaving "Not for nothing Mr Duncan, but could you ask your friend to come out of the bathroom before we leave so that we can see who she is?" Donald hesitated for a few seconds and when he couldn't come up with a reason not to comply, he yelled "Gladys would you please come out of the bathroom. There are some parole officers here who want to speak to you." A few more minutes passed and since there was no response from the bathroom, Terrance and Sherry looked at each other and simultaneously but with caution moved toward the bathroom door. Terrance knocked on bathroom door and yelled, "Whoever is in there needs to come out" as Sherry pulled her 38! When there still was no response finding the door locked Terrance kicked it. His second kick forced the door open. Standing in the bath tub fully dressed was an unidentified man who upon seeing Sherry pointing a gun at him started hollering frantically at the top of his voice while shielding his face with his left hand. Sherry ordered him in a loud voice to take his right hand out of his pocket. He didn't comply still screaming hysterically. Terrance took a chance and jumped into the bathtub where he pulled the man's hands from his pocket, and then quickly jumped back out of the tub. In that hand the man held a Bic lighter. Seeing the lighter and not sure if Sherry did, he yelled at her "It's a lighter - it's a lighter, don't shoot!" When he was sure that his partner had taken her finger off the trigger he climbed back in the tub and handcuffed the man. The man in the tub had no identification on him and refused to tell the officers his name. He was consequently taken to the local police precinct where it was determined that he was a parole violator by the name of Henry Moore. When they read the arrest card that the police had on file it indicated that while in prison Mr Moore had been in protective custody because he was a known homosexual and pedophile preferring the company of underaged boys. Later Sherry shared with her partner that it was a good thing he was there to jump into the tub because she was going to blow him away if he didn't take his hand out of his pocket.

CHAPTER 10

"SHERRY'S OBSESSION"

Sherry continued to be obsessive about finding Champion. At times she was called on the carpet because she was spending so much time looking for him that she was neglecting her other cases. Her Bureau Chief, who was her supervisor's boss, however, defended her actions because he knew that if this man was arrested by his parole officers it would make him look good. Politics always seemed to Terrance, to play a part in the decisions that the administrators made. Terrance didn't mind because he was racking up a ton of hours in overtime pay. What Sherry was patiently waiting for finally happened. Champion's sister informed her that her brother was seen hanging out in the Queensbridge area of Queens, New York. Sherry immediately wanted to saddle up and follow up on the information. What she didn't want to do was bring enough back up to be safe. She was concerned that since she could not trust everyone in the office she did not want the information to be leaked back to Champion. She decided to share this information with only a few people. She thought that Champion had not been caught because he was warned some of the times they were close to catching him. This was the first time Terrance came in touch with the fact that the parole agency really needed to push the internal investigation. She and Terrance argued vehemently over the issue of back up, since they thought the lead was credible. She finally agreed to contact Ollie and Jimmy to back them up. Terrance wanted more but he went along with the compromise. He knew that if they spotted Champion he could call for more help over his radio.

The four officers rode up and down the streets in the Queensbridge area in two unmarked cars looking for Champion. While riding down one of the streets, Sherry from the passenger seat, spotted Champion standing on a corner with about fifteen other people. When Terrance heard her say in an excited voice, "There he is," he quickly drove away from the corner before she could jump from the vehicle. He wasn't sure that she was going to jump out of the car, but he wasn't taking any chances. He remembered his past thought that one mistake could prove fatal. By the time their car got to the end of the block Sherry had informed Ollie and Jimmy over her police radio. The four officers met a block away to decide how to approach this dangerous situation. Terrance wanted to call for more back up now that their quarry had been sighted. Sherry didn't want to wait for fear that he would escape before the backup arrived. Jimmy suggested that the four officers in their two cars watch him from different vantage points and make a decision on how to proceed over their radios. They consequently parked in two different locations where they could see Champion. Terrance immediately suggested that they not approach the area because there were at least 15 people out there and he didn't know what they were carrying in the way of weapons. He assumed that Champion was armed. Jimmy responded that he thought they should just watch him and see if he separates himself from the crowd. It was 6pm on a hot summer evening so the officers knew that they had at least two more hours of day light left. Terrance was glad his car had air conditioning because he was sweating profusely in his bullet proof vest. Some of that sweat was the by product of his fear of what was about to take place. He was glad that he was sitting in the car with Sherry, because he didn't think that Ollie or Jimmy could slow her down. She was anxious to go. The officers watched the corner intently for about 45 minutes when Jimmy radioed that he thought they had waited long enough so he was going to call for back up. Within minutes of his radio transmission Champion and two other men who were in the crowd began to walk away, after talking to a third man who appeared on the scene. Without giving the situation any further thought Sherry jumped from the car saying," I'm not going to let this motherfucker get away." Champion spotted her and immediately took off running as did the other men with him. Terrance had no choice but to follow his partner out of the car. Ollie and Jimmy saw Champion run and sped off in their car, in an attempt to cut the men off in the next block. While riding in the car Jimmy radioed in a 1013 which was the police code for officer needing immediate assistance. As he and Ollie reached the next corner they saw Champion and the other two men cross the street and run into a house that appeared to be abandoned. All four officers reached the front of the building at the same time. Ollie jumped from his car and started running into the building with Sherry close behind. She yelled for Jimmy and Terrance to "Cover the back!" As they reached the back of the house they saw one of the men coming out of a basement door. Jimmy yelled "Police stop!" The man turned and fired two shots at him. Jimmy and Terrance returned fire from about twenty five feet away hitting him in both legs with five out of eight shots. As the man fell he dropped his gun to the ground. Terrance quickly moved in picked up the gun, flipped him over on his stomach, and then handcuffed him, as Jimmy covered him. The kid who appeared to be no more than seventeen years old was now screaming loudly "You shot me! You shot me you bastards!" Terrance looked down at him and sarcastically said "Little boys shouldn't play with guns." At this time both officers heard gun shots coming from inside the house, at the same time they also heard police sirens coming in their direction. When Jimmy got no response on the radio from Ollie the men decided to enter the building. They used their flashlights in the dark hot building to light their way, cautiously watching where they walked as their guns moved in the same directions as their heads. Terrance yelled out Sherry's name and did not receive any response. By the time he yelled out to her for the third time getting no response he had a sinking feeling in his stomach, like something was wrong. The officers worked their way to the second floor of the house sweeping each room for danger as they worked their way down the hall. They observed that some of the rooms looked lived in. When they reached the last room at the end of the hall everything that Terrance feared was now reality. Sherry was lying on the floor motionless with her head leaning against the wall, as if she was sleep. Ollie was five feet away lying facedown on the floor. Jimmy frantically screamed into his radio that two officers were down on the second floor rear room. He then scanned the room with his gun for anyone else who might be friend or foe before going to check on his partner. Terrance lifted Sherry's head off the wall and cradled it in his lap. He began talking to her "You can't die," he said. "You have two beautiful girls to raise." He then saw two bullet holes in her sweat shirt, but no blood. He pulled up her shirt and saw where the bullets entered but still no blood. Before he could search further more police and medical staff entered the room. One of the paramedics rushed over to Sherry and told Terrance to move out of the way so that she could do her job. As Terrance got up from the floor he told the technician that it didn't appear as if the bullets penetrated her body. He stood there watching the examination trying to be tough, when he was told by the paramedics that it didn't appear that the bullets touched Sherry's body but her throat had been cut and she was not breathing. The paramedic was then assisted by another technician as they tried to revive her. After about ten minutes one of them looked at the other and said,"She's gone." At that moment Terrance looked down at Sherry's lifeless body, tears now streaming down his face, and felt that at that moment they were the only people in the room. Ollie had already been pronounced dead. He then looked down and realized that his pants were soaked with blood, Sherry's blood. He still couldn't believe that this had happened. He got angry with her for a minute thinking, "I told you this guy was dangerous! Why didn't you listen to me?" He was briefly pulled out of his tunnel vision by a police captain who first asked him was he alright, and then for the revolver that he used on the kid in the backyard. He did have the presence of mind to also give the captain the gun he took from the kid. Although he nodded yes to the Captain's question he knew he wasn't alright his partner had just been killed.

The police throughly searched the building and did not find Champion or the other man. They did find a rope ladder hanging out of a window on the third floor left side of the building. They figured that this was how the men escaped. Parole officers were now arriving on the scene. Hearing the bad news about Sherry, they turned their attention to Terrance to make sure he was alright, or even if he wasn't they could give their support. Terrance's Bureau Chief ordered him to go to the hospital to be checked out even though Terrance told him he was alright. The Bureau Chief was a political animal, but he cared about the officers he commanded. On the way to the hospital all types of thoughts consumed Terrance's mind. How do I tell Sherry's husband that she is dead and there was nothing that I could have done to prevent it, given the circumstances surrounding the situation? Can I ever face Sherry's daughters who look so much like her? What do I do now? It suddenly dawned on him that the actions he was just involved with would grab immediate media attention. He asked his fellow officers to pull over so that he could call his wife on the phone to let her know he was alright. When talking to his wife on the phone he felt guilty informing her that he was fine but that Sherry was dead.

Terrance agreed the next day after talking to his supervisor and union representative, to be interviewed by the police and parole officials. He and Jimmy were quickly found not to have done anything wrong and were restored to active duty. Terrance may have not been found guilty by his parole agency of doing anything wrong, but he felt guilty. He questioned his lack of effort in being more forceful in stopping his partner's actions. He questioned over and over what he could have done differently. It bothered him to the point that he had difficulty sleeping.

Terrance went to Sherry's home to visit with her husband and children. Through his tears he told her husband Phil how distressed and guilty he felt about Sherry's untimely death. To ease some of his pain her husband told him that he knew his wife was consumed with finding Champion. That was all that she talked about during their pillow talk. He explained to Terrance how he tried to discourage her from being obsessed with finding that man, and how it was affecting their relationship and her relationship with her children. You knew Sherry he said. Once she locked in on something she couldn't let it go. Finally he told Terrance that he didn't blame him for her death, but hoped that he would leave no stone unturned in finding her killer. Before leaving the home the two men hugged and Phil whispered in Terrance's ear, "Go get um for Sherry." Terrance promised that he would do just that.

The other person in Terrance's life, who was concerned about his mental health after the trauma he had just suffered was his wife Camille. It didn't bother her that there was a police car parked in front of her home seven days a week, or that she was escorted and picked up from school everyday by parole officers, who volunteered for the job. It did bother her a bit that her daughter had to be transported to and from day care by armed police and parole officers. She accepted these things as the cost of doing business on the job her husband chose. She, however, did worry about how the tragic incident was affecting Terrance.

Terrance came home late one night after working on Sherry's case to find Camille waiting up for him. "Can we talk"she asked? Terrance, although he was tired said yes. He couldn't refuse to talk to the woman who had been in his corner through all that had happened recently and before. He uncorked a bottle of merlot and the two of them sat on the floor in their bedroom for a talk. Camille explained to her husband that she was afraid that he was cutting her off. You haven't talked to me or anyone else that I know of since Sherry's death. I spoke to your father who I know that you talk to all the time, and even he has not heard from you. Terrance admitted that she was right. I apologize for my behavior, and I didn't do it on purpose, but I can't erase Sherry's lifeless body from my mind. All I think about is catching the bastard that cut her throat. I need you to support my actions now as you have done on many occasions in the past. I won't rest until Sherry's killer is either caught or killed. If I'm worried about you and Tiana then it will make it more difficult for me to do what I feel that I have to do. I can't tell you what I'm doing, partly because I don't want you to know for safety reasons. Second, I don't always know what I'm going to do myself. Camille told Terrance that if she didn't love him she wouldn't have put up with what she had already gone through as a result of Sherry's death. She didn't liked being closed off. "You know I've got your back," she said. I am just concerned that you would prefer to see Sherry's killer dead rather than caught! You have worked so hard to do the righteous things with your life, so I'm afraid that you might now be losing your soul. It is important for you to remember that your family needs you too, especially you daughter. No matter how bad things get in a child's life, they are better off with a father than without one. If a couple agree's on everything, that suggests that they are operating on only one brain. That's not us, she said. She then urged him to do what he had to do, now that she had said her piece. They spent the rest of the night holding each other in bed. It was the best sleep Terrance had since Sherry's death.

CHAPTER 11

"FULFILLING HER WISH"

Terrance requested that he be allowed to speak at Sherry's funeral. They had been partners for the past three years and he was the last Parole Officer to see her alive, so who could deny his request. It was a beautiful sunny morning in August. If there was such a thing as a nice day for a funeral, it was that type of day. Terrance sat with the other adminstrators who were asked to speak among the 200 people in attendence. After Sherry's family filed in to the church, her husband walked over to Terrance, who was sitting next to his wife Camille, and asked them to please come and sit with the family. As Terrance sat in the church next to Sherry's mother who was consoling one of her grandaughters, he was hoping that his speech would help rid himself of some of the guilt that was eating at him. Camille knowing how he felt about what happened, and watching his reactions to everything that was happening in the church squeezed his hand to let him know that she knew what he was going through. He turned and looked at her and she whispered in his ear, "I understand." When Terrance spoke he talked about Sherry's tenacious nature. He spoke about the soft side of her personality, which she didn't share with most people. He ended his speech by talking about how important he felt that it was that we as a community take back the neighborhood Sherry died trying to protect. He looked down from the podium at Sherry's coffin and promised her that he would apprehend the animal that did this to you.

Terrance requested to be involved in the investigation into Sherry's murder. The agency denied his request, and also stopped him from continuing to look for Champion. He was urged by the agency to take some time off because of the post tramatic stress usually associated with the incident he had just experienced. He told his Bureau Chief that unless he was ordered to take time off he wanted to continue working. He did resume working, but was ordered to turn over all information that he and Sherry had put together, in their attempts to apprehend Champion. He didn't like it but Terrance understood why he was taken off the case. He knew that he was now too close personally to the case. He also knew that in order for him to absolve himself of some of the guilt he felt that he had to be involved in catching Champion, so he said the hell with agency policy. He made copies of everything he had before turning the papers over to the new officers assigned the case. Catching Sherry's killer was worth taking the risk of losing his job. I can find another job, but first I have to be able to live with myself. She would have done no less for him, he thought. He telephoned some of his street contacts and told them no matter what they were instructed to do by any other law enforcement agency he wanted to be kept in the loop. He reminded them, and there were many because of the way he had treated them all. They owed him favors, which he was now calling in. During his unauthorized investigation sometimes he would go to other parole offices in the Bronx and Brooklyn, where he was not known, on their reports days and sit in the waiting rooms quietly in disguise to hear the chatter. He knew that parolee's talked about what was going on in the street while waiting to be seen by their parole officers.

Fortunately Terrance was assigned a new partner who was of like mind. Sonny Simms had been a parole officer for five years. He was a six foot tall, slender black man, who carried himself in a way that told you not to mess with him. He was an expert shot and a black belt in karate. Both men's background in the study of marshal arts connected them immediately. Sonny was respected by both the parole officers and the parolees.

The new partners went out for drinks shortly after their partnership began. While sitting in a bar Terrance shared with Sonny what he was about to do. He told him that he was going to work the case sometimes on his own time. He explained to his new partner that he was not going to let anyone or anything stop him from trying to catch Champion. He owed Sherry that much. "It's the only way I can get rid of the pain that I feel," he said. Sonny knew and admired Sherry, so he had no problem with helping where he could. The two men decided to confide their intentions to their supervisor, off the record. They felt he could be trusted and might be able to help them behind the scene. They also knew that he loved and respected Sherry as parole officer. When they approached the supervisor about backing what they were about to do, as they hoped for, he gave them on the record advice, and off the record advice. Off the record he gave them his blessing. On the record he told them he knew what they were thinking and advised them to stay out of it. He warned them that they could lose their jobs if things went wrong, to which Terrance replied "Nuff said."

Every law enforcement agency in the New York area joined the hunt for Champion after the murder of the two officers. They now didn't just want to catch him, they also wanted to destroy his whole organization. Before Terrance was taken off the case he was invited by Jimmy to a warehouse in Brooklyn which was the command center for the task force assigned to the Champion case. There were over fifty officers from the NYPD, New York State Police, FBI, DEA, and IRS all assigned to work the case around the destruction of Champion's crime empire. They had already taken into custody several of the top people in the crime family, and over a hundred of the organization's street dealers. Most of the arrests were for minor offenses but these offenses were enough to get them off the street and maybe get someone to talk. As Terrance walked around the warehouse he saw some information written on push pin boards that he was already aware of and he took mental notes on some of the things that he didn't know. It occurred to him after seeing all of the information gathered in this building that he had one contact that he was sure no one had interviewed..

Terrance made a call to the one person that owed him a favor and could probably get results quicker than anyone else. He called Pauly and asked that they meet. The two men met for breakfast at an out of the way place in Manhattan. When Pauly walked into the diner near the Jacob Javits center he immediately told Terrance that with the help of his crew he made sure he wasn't followed. He knew that if his former parole officer wanted to meet with him it was serious. He said he was sorry to hear about what happened to Sherry. He admitted that every time he saw her he was turned on sexually. "Now how the hell can I help you?" Terrance told him that he knew that he had his hands in the drug trade so he wanted him to help him locate Champion. He didn't care what Pauly had to do to get the information, "just get it." Even if he couldn't find him Terrance wanted to be pointed in the right direction. Pauly first responded to this request with a smile on his face. He couldn't believe that the "choir boy" was asking for his help. Terrance further explained that he felt that sometimes in order to achieve good you have to do evil. This was one of those times. They had a late breakfast of bacon, eggs, home fries and Bloody Marys, after which Pauly picked up the check. Before leaving he assured Terrance that he would do what he could.

As Terrance drove back to Queens he thought to himself, that he was becoming what he never wanted to become. He had an epiphany that suggested that there were people in the world who were just evil. They can't and don't want to be changed. He felt now that they should be destroyed for the sake of the innocent. He wasn't thinking about helping anyone. Social work be damned. All he wanted to do now was find the animal that killed his partner. He was losing his humanity. The side of him he had always been afraid to unleash was loose. It was now out of the bag and Terrance wasn't trying to push it back. He was now the officer that he hated. Sherry's obsession was now Terrance's obsession.

His next plan of action was to find out what parole's internal affairs people were doing about the people in the agency, that he heard were under investigation. He and Sonny both thought that these people were dragging their feet on the investigation so they decided to push them. Sonny had developed a relationship with one of the investigators, so he got her to meet with both he and Terrance alone. Dorothy Paulin was a white woman in her mid fifties who was only a few years from retirement. She took the job in internal affairs because at her age she thought it safer than chasing 19 year olds around their neighborhoods. She owed Sonny a few favors as he had helped her solve some cases concerning corrupt parole officers in the past. The three people met, as Terrance did with Pauly, in an out of the way restaurant. Terrance wanted to know why nothing was being done concerning the suspected corrupt parole officers, especially since most of the people in the Queens office had some idea of who the people were under investigation. Off the record Dorothy told the men that the major target of her investigation was Nikita Novofastovsky. Nikita was of European decent, born in Bosnia and migrated to America as a young child. According to Dorothy, and through rumors, he had no allegiance to parole or anyone else. He took the job as an officer strictly for the money, and made that clear to everyone. He had a folder of write ups for negative behavior the size of a paper back novel, but had never been suspended or punished for his behavior. Dorothy was trying to ascertain why. She told the men that she felt that part of the reason he was never penalized or disciplined for his behavior was simply because he was white. She was aware of black and Hispanic officers who were suspended or fired for simular offenses. Nikita joined the agency just before a federal law suit forced New York State Parole to hire more women and people of color. This made him a part of the good old boys network. She further informed them that he was suspected of having ties to the round table drug organization. The problem she was having was getting anyone in that organization to talk, and he had been smart enough to avoid detection. She told her lunch guests that she had checked Novofastovsky financials, and that although he also worked as a private detective, part time, he had more money in his accounts than a person in those professions should have unless he received it through some other means. He explained to her during questioning about his finances that the money was part of the retainers he received from clients in his investigation business. By law he did not have to reveal the names of his clients. It was also discovered that he had been seen in some of the other parole offices in the Bronx and Manhattan days before a couple of rival gang members were shot and killed in their homes. He was suspected of imparting address information to the round table gang, but it hadn't been proven. Terrance didn't like this man anyway because he was one of the officers who avoided helping him when he started on the job. He always impressed Terrance as someone who thought himself smarter than everyone else, especially black people. These reasons made it easy for him to direct some of his anger at Nikita Novofastovshy.

After the meeting, Terrance reached out to Jimmy to see what he could find out about Novofastovsky from police files. Within days Jimmy told him that Nikita was suspected of having ties to the Russian mob. He then warned him to be careful. Terrance began to wonder how this guy was able to survive in the law enforcement world while under suspicion for so many serious offenses. Who is getting paid to look the other way? Terrance thought it more dangerous to challenge who ever had his back than to worry about him.

Sonny thought it better to start their investigation from inside the office. They casually talked to the staff about Nikita. They found out that he was in the office on the day that Sherry was murdered. Terrance then remembered he and Sherry talking to their supervisor about their plans based on the tip they received on Champion's possible whereabouts. The supervisor instructed the two officers to contact him immediately if Champion was spotted. He didn't want to commit other officers to the surveillance as he had done so many times in the past several weeks only to come up with negative results. Terrance now wished that he had followed those instructions in spite of any objections that Sherry had. He wondered that since they had talked with the office door open, which was not unique, did Nikita over hear any of the conversation. He thought back to the evening of the incident and realized that Champion was constantly talking on the phone in a nearby phone booth and that just before he fled he was approached by a man who whispered something in his ear. He gave this information to Jimmy in the hopes that the task force would check the numbers called from that booth on that night and around that time.

While waiting for the results from Jimmy, the partners decided to shadow Nikita for a couple of days. Terrance borrowed his wife's car and Sonny used the car of a friend so that Nikita would not automatically spot his followers. On the second day of following him they were called to the office so they broke off the surveilance. When they arrived at the parole office they were informed that the police and parole internal affairs were there to talk with Nikita. He was also called to the office and arrived a few minutes after them. Jimmy was there in the office with the investigating detectives. He took Terrance and Sonny into their office, closed the door and told them that three calls were made to the phone booth in question from their parole office on the date, and around the time of the incident. Nikita was the prime suspect but everyone in the office that day had to be questioned, which was procedure. He further told the men that they weren't going to be interviewed because Terrance naturally was not in the office at that time. He couldn't be in two places at once, and Sonny didn't work in the Queens Field Office at the time. Jimmy was hoping that someone would force Nikita to crack, but he knew it was going to be hard. Terrance didn't need confirmation of who warned Champion, he now knew. He also now felt that this guy was the key to finding his prey. He began thinking and then talking to Sonny about what he wanted to do. If no one was able to box Nikita into a corner where he would be forced to give up any information that he had concerning Champion's whereabouts he would have to do it himself. Sonny urged Terrance to think about his career. He told him to remember that he had a family to support. "How are you going to give your daughter all you told me that you wanted to give her if you lose your job or even worse end up in jail or dead?" He said that he would continue to back his play, but he wanted him to be smart in his decision making. Sonny didn't want Terrance to be led purely by his emotions, that's what got Sherry killed. Terrance thought that this was the same type of advice that Billy gave him when they were in college. The task force spent a couple days interviewing and re-interviewing some people who were in the office that day. Nikita didn't crack, and they were unable to prove that he made the calls. Terrance was now as angry as he had been since the evening Sherry died. "It's not what you know it's what you can prove," was not good enough for him. Math was not Terrance's favorite subject but he was sure that two plus two equaled four. To make it even worse he didn't know who to trust beyond three or four people in his office. There were some secretaries in the office who were also under investigation for being involved with the drug gang. He now wanted Nikita's ass and he was going to get it in spite of the circumstances. Nikita was under a microscope now, and he knew it, so he became cautious in his activities. Terrance decided that it would take more than police legal activities to get him to talk. Since he was drawing a blank everywhere else he decided to meet with Pauly again for suggestions. He needed advice on working outside the law and not getting caught. He thought Pauly to be a master at accomplishing that goal.

The two men met at a different restaurant this time in New Jersey. Terrance brought his criminal minded friend up to date on what he knew and asked for advice. He didn't want Sonny to know what he might plan because he didn't want him to jeopardize his job. Pauly told Terrance that he was sure Champion was getting inside help avoiding being captured but he wasn't sure if Nikita was the leak. He went on to say that although Nikita had some connections to the Russian mob it was not significant enough for them to protect him. Pauly felt it better not to tell Terrance that he also wanted Champion caught. His organization was being affected by the heat the task force was putting on everyone in his business, because they wanted Champion and his organization destroyed, so it was the ripple affect. Once Champion was caught Pauly could get back to business. He rationalized that he could pay a debt, and eliminate a problem at the same time. Pauly finally told Terrance that he had some ideas on what he could do. He thought it best that "the choir boy" not know what he was planning. He promised that if Nikita knew anything, that he would get it out of him.

CHAPTER 12

"STAY OUT OF THE INVESTIGATION"

It was a rainy humid evening, and Nikita was going about his business visiting the homes of his parolees. Although he had been cautious, now aware that he was suspected of criminal activity, he relaxed a bit thinking, even if he was being watched now he wasn't doing anything wrong. He can't be arrested for doing his job, he thought. After visiting the home of one of his parolees he was walking down the driveway when a huge white man exited a black cadilac, crossed the street and appeared to be approaching him. Nikita suspected that since this man was white in an African American neighborhood he must be a cop. Consequently he thought to himself "What the hell does he want now?" The man greeted Nikita by saying "Hey I need to talk to you." When the man got within a foot of Nikita he pulled a small pistol from his waistband and shoved it in to Nikita's stomach, while at the same time saying in a soft voice "Come with me." Nikita was shocked at this action but he wasn't going to argue with someone who had a gun pushed against his stomach and then his ribs. Once the men reached the Caddy, the door opened and another man reached out and took Nikita's service revolver from under his vest. He was then pushed into the back seat of the car where he sat between two men who he knew through their silence meant business. He quickly realized that these men were not cops. He took a chance and asked them where they were taking him? The man who originally approached him responded "You'll see!" Nikita tried to look out of the windows to get some idea of where he was going but he found it difficult because it was now dark outside and the car windows where blacked out. The misty rain didn't help either. He didn't feel smarter than anyone else now. He realized that he was in big trouble.

He was driven to an industrial area near Shea Baseball Stadium and taken into a building where he observed several cars in need of body work. The building was dark and damp and the only light available was from the flashlights his escorts were carrying. One of the men took his handcuffs from his belt, motioned for him to place his hands behind his back and then handcuffed him. Nikita had no idea what was happening but he thought it in his best interest to comply. Without any of the men saying a word he was led to a chair where he was forced to sit down. Feeling anxious and now worried, he once again asked "What is this all about?" No one answered him. He thought he was protected from problems with the drug gang, but these men were a different breed, because they were white. He never considered having problems with another mob. During the next several minutes no one in the room said a word. He heard the sound of a barking dog, which had been placed in a cage when he was led into the building. He heard the sound of passing trains. He thought that they might be Long Island Railroad trains, that pass through that area, but there was no conversation between the men who brought him to this building. Suddenly the door opened and a slightly built tall man entered the room. He shook the rain from his umberella while closing it. He then walked to within ten feet of Nikita and asked him a question, "Do you know Ronald Champion Duncan?" Nikita hesitated and then responded "I know who he is." With that response one of the men in the room came up behind him, wrapped a belt around his neck and yanked it cutting off his ability to breathe. Nikita struggled for breath while his legs flailed in the chair. The slender man nodded to the strangler, who then released his grip on the belt. He then said, "Now I am going to repeat the question, "Do you know Ronald Champion Duncan?" Clearing his throat and twisting his head to catch his breath, he answered "Yes I know him." The slender man then told Nikita that he would save himself a lot of pain if he answered questions asked truthfully, and not bullshit him. That being said, he asked Nikita "Where is Champion?" Nikita responded that answering that question could get him killed. The slender man told Nikita "You had better look around and see where you are now." Nikita quickly scanded the room barely able to see through the darkness. "If you give me the information that I want, you will leave here alive and can make your own plans to get ahead of the situation," the slender man then stated. Nikita hesitated and again the belt was rapped around his neck choking him. This time along with the choking, another man in the room quickly kicked him in the balls causing additional pain. Although these activities only lasted seconds, to Nikita this pain lingered much longer. The slender man asked him again, "Where is Champion?" Just before the henchmen moved in again Nikita yelled "OK, OK, listen, I don't know where Champion is now, because he moves around." Sensing that Nikita had more to tell, and was not good at enduring pain, he asked "What else can you tell me?" "He calls me for information," Nikita

Quickly responded. "He does however have a couple of men that I can contact who will get a message to him. "I want names, and the ways you make contact with these guys," the unnamed, no nonsense, man responded. "Oh yeah!" "If the information that you give me proves to be bullshit, my associates and I will be visiting you again, and the next time you will wish for the pain that you felt this time. You don't want to see us again, I promise you!" Nikita told him that their names were Calvin "Smitty" Smith and Troy Williams. He also told him how to get in touch with them. The cuffs were consequently taken off Nikita and then he was driven back to his car. Before the three silent men released him, one of them shoved a hundred dollar bill in the chest pocket of his vest, and said "Thanks for the info just don't make me have to come take the money back!" As he watched the Cadillac drive away, for the first time Nikita realized how much danger he was in, because if the round table found out he had snitched they would kill him. If the men who just dropped him off, weren't satisfied with the information he gave them, and they came back, he might be thankful for death. Finally he was sure that the cops were doing everything that they could to link him to Champion's organization. He was now truly scared.

Terrance was given this information through an envoy of Pauly's. He and Sonny were familiar with Calvin Smith. Although he was currently a parole absconder, the five foot tall, muscle man with a long criminal record for minor offenses was affable. Many of the parole officers, in the Queens Parole office, liked him because he would entertain them with stories about stupid criminals like himself. One female parole officer described him as "Cute and Cuddly." He probably could have made it as a comedian if not for his inability to stay away from crime. Terrance never considered him dangerous, only amusing. Smitty was an expert at picking pockets. Terrance never told him so, but he admired the skill that it took for someone to commit this type of crime. He thought about the hours of practice and dedication it takes to become an expert. Practice makes perfect. Parole Officers tried to convince Smitty that if he used that same dedication to do something positive for himself he would be successful. He knew what they were trying to tell him made sense, but he was comfortable in the criminal world.

Terrance once over heard a conversation between Smitty and another parolee while they were in the parole office. The two men were talking about their plans for New Years Eve. They were going to the Times Square area of Manhattan, to allegedly watch the ball drop. They talked about how many people would be there for the event, and how much fun they were going to have. Hearing this conversation, and knowing that if these two men went to this area, at that time, with thousands of people walking around, this would be fertile ground for them to commit crimes, especially pick pocketing. He consequently with the help of their parole officers forbade them from going there. He further told both men that he was going to call their places of residence at midnight to make sure they were home. He didn't make the calls that night because he was having too much fun himself, but he knew that the threat of incarceration was a strong incentive to follow his directives.

One could conclude from Smitty's stories that he was entrenched in the culture of the street. Troy Williams was an unknown quantity, so Terrance gave his name to Jimmy for further investigation. Like Terrance, Jimmy was ordered to stay out of the investigation. Like Terrance he wasn't going to follow those orders, unless he saw quicker results in solving the murder of his partner. Since Terrance and Sonny had information through parole on Calvin they decided to focus their attention on finding him. They also figured that they could justify going after him simply because he was a parole violator. No one in New York State Parole except the partners and their supervisor seem to know there was a link between him and Champion. Since they had addresses where he might be found, they enlisted the help of two other parole officers they thought they could trust to back them up on apprehending him. At about six in the morning the four officers went to the small ranch style home, where he was supposed to be living with his girlfriend. Just as the sun was rising Terrance rang the door bell, after asking the female member of his back up team, to watch the back of the house in case he tried to exit that way. A large elderly woman, who was walking with the assistance of a cane, answered the door and after the officers identified themselves she told them that Smitty was in the house, sleeping in the bedroom with her grandaughter. The old woman didn't appear to know that Smitty was wanted, so she let the three officers in the house and pointed out her grandaughter's bedroom, which was in the back of the house. Upon approaching the bedroom door they heard the sounds of a woman moaning in ecstasy. Sonny looked at Terrance, smiled and whispered, "Sounds like the funny man is in there getting his groove on." He then tried to turn the door knob, only to find the door locked. Consequently Terrance then yelled "Smitty we know you are in there, so unlock the door and let us in!" There was no response to this directive, only the faint sound of whispers, and no more moaning. Terrance then said "To hell with this," and began kicking on the door. Sonny joined in, and together the door was forced open as the door frame splintered into pieces. As they entered the room they heard the female officer who was outside radio to them that Smitty was coming out of the window. She then grabbed him around the neck from behind, as he tried to run away, forcing both of them to the ground. Smitty managed to break free of her grip as they rolled over, and in one swift move jumped over a five foot backyard fence. This was the first of several consecutive backyard fences that he scaled as he ran through yard after yard. Terrance followed him out of the window as his girlfreind screamed, "Don't hurt him!" He reached the ground just in time to grab the arm of the female officer and pull it down before she took a shot at Smitty, as he yelled "Don't shoot him! I need him alive!" She was pissed off that he got away from her, but complied with Terrance's command. Terrance then noticed that as Smitty was making his escape all he was wearing was a pair of pants; no underpants, no shirt, socks or shoes, and even more importantly a belt to hold up his pants. Avoiding capture was more important than dressing. As he hit the ground after climbing over each wire fence, his pants would fall down to his knees exposing his bare ass, as he continued to flee. Watching this from a distance, Terrance started to laugh. For a moment he forgot about his anger and any danger he might have faced. Sonny called over the radio for police help as he ran back to the front of the house, climbed into his car, and attempted to cut off Smitty's retreat at the end of the block. Unfortunatly for the officers, although they knew the area well Smitty, knew it better, escaping through a back alley. Sonny told Terrance, after Smitty's escape, that he thought he would return to the residence. He was bare-foot, shirtless, and like most people on parole, creatures of habit. Terrance agreed, adding that he was also going to miss the trim he was getting in the bedroom.

The two PO's (parole officers) decided to sit on the residence and wait for Smitty's return. They sat on the residence for the next couple of days without any results. They observed people coming and going from the house, but no signs of Smitty, so they called off the surveillance. They also could not afford to be accused of neglecting their other cases.

At the end of the second day they went back to their office and were informed that PO Novofastovsky was missing. He hadn't reported to work in three days, and his live in girlfriend told parole administration that he had not been home. None of his clothes were missing, and none of his friends had seen him in the past few days. Terrance got a bit nervous after hearing this information. Even though his

Italian contacts assured him that when Nikita was released he was in good health, other than a few marks around his neck and between his legs. It was thought by many of the parole officers in the office, who suspected him of playing both sides against the middle, that his behavior finally caught up with him. No one, not even Sonny, knew about Terrance's connection to Pauly. His anger however still over ruled his concern about getting in trouble. He still saw what he was doing as a reckoning for Sherry. Parole administration and the police were aware of Novofastovsky possible links to the drug gang so they had duel purpose for finding him.

Over the course of the next several days Terrance found out that the other man who escaped with Champion was identified as Byron Becks. He was a dangerous man with a criminal history dating back to the age of 12. He was rumored to have shot and killed his father at the age of 15, after watching his mother be beaten unconscious, although he was never charged with the crime. He worked his way up through the ranks to become a collector of money for the drug gang, and when employees didn't pay or came up short he was the gang's enforcer. The task force issued a warrant for his arrest in connection with the deaths of Sherry and Otis.

Terrance and Sonny continued to follow up on the leads that they were given. It was as though Champion had disappeared from the face of the earth, or at least out of the neighborhood. It was as though he left New York, but continued leads suggested he was still around. One time they were told that Champion might be hiding in Howard Beach, Queens, which was a neighborhood made up mostly of people of Italian ancestry. People of a different hue were not always welcome in this neighborhood. Terrance didn't tell anyone why, but knew that the tip wasn't true thanks to Pauly. He had in the past had many discussions with white ex cons who bragged about the fact that they could go into black neighborhoods and commit crimes much easier than a person of color could in a white neighborhood. When a black man walks through a white neighborhood, he is watched constantly by the people from that neighborhood unless he is known to the residence, such as a mailman might be. The minute the black stranger appears to do anything suspicious the police are called, or he is questioned by one of the residences. The standard line was"Can I help you?" Black parole officers had the dubious distinction of being watched by the residents no matter what neighborhood they visited. They were challenged in the white areas and watched with suspicion in the black neighborhoods.

On another occasion the partners got a tip that Smitty was hiding out in the home of another relative. They once again enlisted the help of three parole officers they could trust, one of them being the parole officer who had been assigned the case. They were told by a man that answered the door to the residence, that Smitty was not in the house. They then explained to the gentleman that they had a warrant and wanted to search the house anyway. He agreed and just as Terrance, Sonny and the case officer entered the residence they heard four shots coming from the rear outside of the home. They immediately ran back out the front door and around to the side of the house where they witnessed the two officers who went to cover the rear with their guns drawn, standing over a rottweller dog that they just shot. The dog was bleeding through the mouth with his tongue hanging out, as he gasped for his last breaths of life. One of the officers told Terrance that the dog attacked as they walked to the back of the house. Both Officers fired twice hitting the dog with all four shots. Watching this massive beast laying there dying Terrance reflected back to his recruit training class where he and his classmates were shown films of dogs attacking law enforcement officers, and the damage that they could inflict if they were not put down quickly. Sonny quickly got everyone to regroup and suggested they search the house before the police arrived, as he saw some of the neighbors come out of their homes after hearing the shots, to see what was going on. If Smitty was in the house, they wanted to arrest him before the police arrived, so that they could question him first. Since the shooters were alright, the three men ran back to the front of the house, entered and started searching. They quickly, but cautiously went through every room of the small house and found no signs of Smitty. As they were leaving the residence to greet the cops who just arrived on the scene Sonny looked back at a sofa in a corner of the living room and asked, "Did anyone looked behind that couch?" The response was no, so he proceded to look behind the sofa. As he pulled it out away from the wall he said to his partners in the search, "Damn that's a heavy couch." Not finding anyone behind the couch Terrance went to help him push it back against the wall. As he aided his partner in pushing, he noticed that the pillows on the couch were uneven. He then used hand signals to let Sonny and the case officer know that he thought someone was inside the sofa. The officers pulled their guns as Terrance flipped back the pillows and pulled out the couch, which was a sofa bed. To their amazement there was a man curled up in the sofa. To their disappointment it wasn't Smitty. Sonny grabbed the man by the collar with his weak hand and yanked him out of the sofa bed. The man was then handcuffed and led out of the house. The man was not identified as anyone that parole wanted so he was turned over to the police who were now investigating the "shots fired" report. It turned out that the reason the man hid was because he had an open bench warrant for his arrest. None of the parole officers involved in the search had ever experienced someone hiding in a fold up sofa before. That was one for the books. Both Sonny and Terrance were frustrated because they felt they were no closer to finding Smitty or Champion. Terrance, who was the motivating cheerleader would say "To hell with it! I'm not giving up! They are hiding somewhere, and I'm going to find them!"

CHAPTER 13

"A GOOD LEAD"

As a result of the dog shooting Terrance and Sonny were called to their Bureau Chief's Office. They both thought that they were going to see the chief, because they were involved in the discharge of a weapon, which was standard procedure; so when the entered the chief's office this was what they were expecting. Upon entering the office they saw and greeted their supervisor who was sitting in a corner of the room. The Chief pointed to the two chairs in front of his desk and asked his officers to take a seat. He began his speech by saying that he thought that the partners were two of his best officers. The tone of his voice then changed. Now that being said, I have been hearing rumblings that you two have been looking for Champion Duncan. There are over fifty people on the task force including some of ours working this case. What can you do that they can't? Terrance looked at the Chief and shrugged his shoulders as to agree with him. At the same time he was thinking this is bull shit, if he only knew. Both Terrance and Sonny acted as though they didn't know what their boss was talking about. The Chief wasn't stupid, so he then said, "If what I hear is true, I want you to cease and desist any further investigations into finding Champion." He then asked them if they heard anything on the street about Nikita's disappearance? They both told him no. He didn't forbid them from helping in the execution of parole warrants, which subliminally sent them a message that they could continue what they were doing, as long as they didn't get caught. He ended the speech by telling them to get the hell out of his office. After they walked out of the office it occurred to Terrance that the Chief never asked them directly whether or not they had been working the case? He had played his political positioning perfectly. If his officers suceeded in locating and capturing Champion he could take part of the credit. If they failed and were caught disobeying orders, he was on record as telling them to withdraw their involvement in the case.

All of the parole officers were warned to be careful when doing home visits, in particular they wanted everyone to look for booby traps that the Round Table may have set up to protect some of their drug spots, since the police had been applying pressure all over the neighborhoood. There were stairs leading up to some apartments that had disguised trip wires that would drop broken glass or a nail on the person who tripped the wire. There were steps with false tops on them, and when someone put their weight on that step, it would give, and that person would land on rusty nails. There were also trip wires that electonically released vicious pit bulls from a pin. These dogs were trained not to bark until they were close enough to attack. These were just some of the many traps being used.

Terrance finally got a break when he received a call from Smitty's girlfriend. She was pissed off because she found out that he was screwing another woman, so she was now willing to tell all that she knew. She told Terrance that although she didn't know where Champion was staying, she knew that Smitty was in constant contact with him. He would bring Champion food, alcohol, drugs and women, to his different hideouts, when he asked, she further informed him. The two men had established a series of phone booths and times set up every two days to communicate. She admitted that when she was previously questioned by the task force on the case she lied to them. "I hate cops," she told him. Although she hadn't met her paramour's parole officer before, she had heard good things about him, so she decided to give him the information, rather than the police, who had treated her in a disrespectful manner, on occasions in the past. She gave Terrance the name of Sonia Rodriguez, who lived in a lower East Side Project in Manhattan. She didn't know Ms Rodriguez's apartment number, but was able to give Terrance an address. She also told him that after all she had done for Smitty's ass she was angry and hurt that he would treat her this way. She finally said, "I hope you catch his ass!"

Terrance found out that Sonia Rodriguez was a 25 year old Puerto Rican, who had a few arrests for drug possession and prostitution. He was unsuccessful in contacting Smitty's case officer, so he and Sonny decided to go after Smitty alone. After all they did receive subliminal approval from the chief, and support from their supervisor. On the ride to the projects they discussed the situation and decided to investigate and surveil the surrounding area before making a move to arrest Smitty. These were mainly

Sonny's suggestions, and Terrance had no problem with them because he knew Sonny would keep him from doing something foolish. The projects consisted of several high rise buildings with a lot of constant activity in the court yard between the buildings. Across the street from the projects was a park which appeared to be the hang out spot for some alcoholics and junkies. The partners decided to go into the park and talk with some of its residents since they didn't know what Sonia looked like, or what apartment she lived in. They knew that if they walked into the court yard first, they would easily be spotted as interlopers, and the word would quickly spread through the grapevine, possiblily alerting Smitty if he was there. At the very least it could make Sonia aware of their presence. In the park they found an old wino by the name of Nacio who told them that he knew Sonia Rodriguez. After some negotiations he agreed to point her out for ten dollars and a half gallon of Tokay wine. They agreed to meet the next morning at seven in the morning.

On the way to meet with their contact the next morning Sonny had doubts as to whether the wino would be there, but when they arrived, there he was sitting on his favorite bench. Nacio wasn't going to miss out on an opportunity to get ten bucks and a half gallon of wine. The three men sat in the state car which was positioned so that they could see everyone who left or returned to the projects. While sitting and waiting for Sonia to show her face they talked. Nacio told them that he once had a good job as a computer programmer, but the company folded. He further said that after losing his job everything went down hill from there. He lost his wife, children and his home. The pressure and depression that followed led him to using drugs and alcohol. "I wasn't always a bum," he said. Nacio also told the officers, during their talk, that he wasn't sure what floor Sonia lived on but that many of the floors in her building were controlled by drug dealers and there were tons of booby traps throughout the building. He further said that it was so dangerous in her building that the police didn't go in there unless they absolutely had to. Regular patrols in that building were out of the question, he told them. The officers showed Nacio a picture of Smitty to see if he had been seen in the area. "I've seen a guy who looks like the picture you showed me come out of the building a few times" he told them. Terrance asked him if he was sure it was Smitty? "Sure looked like him. I asked him for some spare change once, and the bastard just blew me off," Nacio answered. The men sat in the car for several hours during which time there were no signs of Smitty or Sonia. They bought Nacio lunch to keep him around but refused to buy him any wine until he identified Sonia. Terrance finally decided that he wanted to go into the building, find the landlord, and get Sonia's apartment number. Sonny agreed as long as they got some police back up, so they drove Nacio to the local liquor store to get him his bottle. When they pulled up next to the liquor store they noticed a NYPD police van sitting across the street by a Duncan Donuts Store. Terrance told Sonny to go buy Nacio his bottle, while he went across the street and asked the police for backup. When he approached the van he noticed that there were no less than seven police officers sitting in the van laughing and joking with each other. There were two more officers in the donut shop. Terrance identified himself and explained to them what he needed. The police officers all looked around at each other for a minute not responding to Terrance's request. During the silence Terrance tried to sweeten the pot by telling them that they didn't have to search the apartment, just watch his back. Someone in the van responded "Hell we're not going in there!" By this time Sonny had completed his transaction with Nacio and walked across the street to see what was going on. Terrance told him that these officers refused to help. Sonny then walked over to the driver, identified himself, and told him to sit still while he contacted a police supervisor, which he did over his police radio. A police sergeant responded to the radio call by telling the officers to stay put until he arrived. Several minutes later a patrol car pulled up and a sergeant got out of the vehicle. Sonny explained to him that he had a warrant for the arrest of someone who might be able to help find the man who killed his fellow officer in Queens. The sergeant then walked up to the van, pointed and said, "You, You, You, and You just volunteered to back these Parole Officers up." He then ordered the van driver to follow Terrance and Sonny back to the apartment building.

When people saw the police van pull up in front of the court yard many of those who were hanging out there scattered. A few of them just stared, as they were shocked to see the police come in to this area. Two of the police officers agreed to watch the entrance to the building, and the other two officers covered the lobby, where the manager's apartment was located. A Hispanic man answered the door and identified himself as the building's manager. He denied ever seeing Smitty, but told them that Sonia Rodriguez lived on the 7th floor, in apartment 7E. The partners decided it was safer to take the elevator than the stairs since they had been warned about the booby traps in the building. They rode to the 7th floor, located apartment 7E, and knocked on the door. An attractive Puerto Rican woman answered the door wearing Daisy Duke Jeans and a halter top. The jeans were so tight, that they left nothing to the imagination. Terrance thought to himself "Damn those jeans are so tight, she might as well not be wearing anything." She didn't appear to understand English so she motioned to the men to come into the apartment and then a have seat. Neither man sat, as Sonny had his hand on his gun in the holster, and Terrance had his hand on his gun in his pocket. A couple of minutes passed when another beautiful Hispanic female walked into the living room and asked if she could help them? The difference between this woman and the one that answered the door, was that this one was naked except for wearing a pair of pink panties. Both men were momentarily distracted. Once Terrance took his eyes off of the more than adequate breasts, which were staring him in the face, he backed himself into a corner thinking someone else might come into the room shooting, while he was lusting over this naked beauty. Sonny was more controlled, he asked the woman her name. She smiled and told him that she was Sonia Rodriguez. Before he could ask another question she asked with a heavy Spanish accent, "Are you looking for Smitty? He ain't here but, I expect that he will be back soon." She further told the officers that she hadn't seen him in a couple days. She offered to allow them to search, but they declined feeling that she was telling the truth. As they left the apartment, seeing that Terrance was aroused by what he just saw, Sonny jokingly told his partner to take his dick out of his pocket and put it back in the holster.

As they rode down in the elevator it stopped on the 3rd floor. A man entered the elevator who looked just like Smitty. He didn't appear spooked, when he saw them as he pushed the elevator button for the lobby. Terrance and Sonny, who were standing behind the man, looked at each other not knowing what to do. Was Smitty that cool under pressure Terrance thought? Hell no! But this man was dressed in a dark suit, and was wearing a tie, which puzzled them. The officers had never seen Smitty dressed this way, but he looked like Smitty; so when the elevator door opened Terrance grabbed the man by the back of his coat jacket and shoved him against a wall in the lobby. While searching him he pulled the man's wallet from his back pocket and tossed it to Sonny. The shocked man asked in a frantic voice after, seeing the two uniform police officers, who were also there in the lobby, "What the hell is going on?" Sonny looked at the identification in the wallet and said to Terrance "Yo man I think you got the wrong person." The man then told the officers that his name was James Smith and that he lived in the building. He said that Smitty was his younger brother. "I moved away from Queens because I was constantly being mistaken for my brother, who is 1 year younger than me," he continued. "I have never been arrested, or had any trouble with the law," he told the officers. He further told the officers that hadn't seen his brother in the past month, but he was aware that he was a frequent visitor to Sonia Rodriguez's apartment. Finally he said "My brother is nothing but trouble, so I stay away from him, and he stays away from me." After checking over their police radio for any wants or warrants which came up negative Terrance apologized to Smitty's brother, while he brushed off the back of his suit jacket, and helped him to straighten his tie. Sonny cautioned his partner to control his temper. "We are on the verge of catching Smitty, so don't screw it up," he said. Terrance didn't respond because he knew Sonny was right. The partners weren't ready to quit now that they had located Smitty's hideout; so they dismissed the cops who were backing them up and went back to sitting in the car, watching the entrance to the building.

Around 5 o'clock they got hungry so Terrance volunteered to walk to a deli he spotted earlier around the corner and get them some food. As he approached the deli he spotted Smitty who was walking into the eatery. He crossed to the other side of the street where he could get a better view of the deli entrance, and called Sonny on his police radio. "I just saw Smitty walk into the deli," he whispered. Sonny responded "Are you sure it's not his brother?" Terrance replied "If it is, he must have changed from the suit we saw him wearing earlier, to short pants dragging off his ass." Sonny drove around the corner and pulled up in front of Terrance who then got into the car. They decided to wait until Smitty exited the store to take him. If there was going to be any gun play they didn't want to do it in a store full of people. Fifteen minutes passed, when they began to think that something was wrong because Smitty had not exited the store. They both then exited their car and went into the store where they saw no sign of Smitty, as they walked up and down the aisles. "Are you sure you saw him come in here," Sonny asked. "I'm positive," Terrance responded. He then went to the cashier and asked to speak to the store manager. Using a Korean dialect, the cashier spoke into an intercom that she had behind her. She then told Terrance in broken English "He coming." While he was waiting for the boss Terrance showed the cashier a picture of Smitty, and asked her had she seen him come into or leave the store. She looked at him with a blank stare, because she didn't understand or speak much English. Just as he was going to ask her again, a small Korean man tapped him on the shoulder and identified himself as the store owner. He said that his name was Quan. Terrance showed the man the photo of Smitty and asked him the same question he did the cashier. The store owner grabbed Terrance by the arm and led him and Sonny to an area in the back of the store that housed four television monitors and four VCR recording machines. He then rewound one of the machines stopping at the place where he wanted them to watch. Terrance and Sonny watched Smitty shoplifting canned goods from the shelves. The time stamped on the TV screen was from ten minutes before they entered the store. Before they could see anymore the owner stopped the tape. He then said in broken English "This man come in to my store and steal one time. I let him go! He come back again and steal. I give him another chance by letting him go! He come back today and steal. "No more chances!!!" The officers then explained that they had a warrant for his arrest. Quan then led them to a hole in the floor in the rear of the building, where he opened what appeared to be a trap door. As soon as the door opened they heard a man screaming in pain. They followed the Korean down the stairs to a basement where they saw Smitty tied in a chair, surrounded by five small Korean men, who were taking turns hitting him in the face and body with broom stick handles and hoses. He yelled with every smack as they kicked his ass. He saw Terrance and immediately pleaded for him for help. "Please PO Jackson." He begged! "Make them stop before they kill me," he yelled! Terrance's first instinct was to save Smitty by stopping the beatings, but he then had and epiphany. What kind of pressure could he put on him legally to get him to give up the information on Champion, he thought? Would he cooperate just because Terrance saved him? Would he cooperate because they previously had a good relationship? He looked at the fear on Smitty's face and thought that right now he was under more pressure than he could ever place on him, unless he planned to do something simular to what the Koreans were currently doing. He wasn't prepared to use physical torture to achieve his goal, although he now saw that as another option. Now thinking this way, he turned and walked up to Smitty passing between the Koreans that surrounded him, and said, "I'll save you only after you answer some questions like, where is Champion?" Smitty looked at him with a blank stare on his face. He didn't expect to be asked that question. Not getting a quick response Terrance walked away from him. The Koreans seeing Terrance turn his back took it as a sign that they could continue whipping on him. Whack! Whack! Whack! Smitty then yelled "Shit man you can't let them do this to me!" Terrance then turned back to him and said, "Do what? I didn't see anything. Sonny did you see anything? " Sonny nodded his head no. "Where is Champion," Terrance asked again? Smitty responded "I don't know!" Sonny then said to Terrance "Hey man, I'm thirsty it's been a long day. Lets go upstairs in the deli and get a couple of beers and a sandwich." As the men climbed the stairs to the store they continued to hear Smitty cry out in pain as he got smacked. The partners were given two beers by Quan which they drank in the back room of the store. While there Sonny asked Terrance "How long are you going to let this continue?" "As long as it takes for him to tell me something," Terrance responded. "Getting hit with broom sticks and hoses must hurt like hell, but won't kill you, at least not right away." After about 15 minutes the men went back to the basement. The old social worker Terrance would at this point have taken pity on Smitty and called the whole thing off. The angry Terrance, who wanted more than anything to capture Champion, dominated the rational thinking social worker, and allowed Smitty to keep getting whupped, in the hope that the results of the beating would created positive results. He knew from talking to Smitty's girlfriend that he had information on Champion, so the question was how much pain would he endure before he gave up something. The Koreans now were taking a break from whipping on Smitty as they were all sitting on the floor still in a circle around Smitty, drinking water and talking in their native tongue. Terrance once again walked around them and up to Smitty who at this point had welts on his face and neck and blood dripping from one nostril. He looked at Terrance shivering from pain and said, "Please help me." Terrance responded, in a soft but stern voice, now more determined than ever to get what he wanted, "Tell me where Champion is and I will get them to stop. I know you are in contact with his ass!" Smitty then told Terrance that he didn't know where Champion was at that moment because he moved around every couple of days. He further told him that he makes contact with him through a series of pay phones in the South Jamaica, Queens area, which they establish each time they talk. He was willing to give Terrance and Sonny the addresses of the phone booths. Sonny told Smitty that he wanted the addresses before he was untied. He then gave the partners the locations of the phone booths, and also told them that occasionally Champion asked him to bring him prostitutes to a couple of hotels that he occasionally stayed in. He also gave them the names and addresses of the hotels, and some other information that they wanted. Since he was now cooperative, Smitty was untied, handcuffed and arrested. He had never been so happy to be arrested. On the way to be turned over to New York City Corrections Terrance suggested to him that it was in his best interest to tell the correction officers that he received his bruises in a fight. "If you tell anyone what actually happened to you, I will make sure that everyone on the street knows where I got my information" he said. "You know that time in jail for a snitch can be dangerous!"

CHAPTER 14

"SPEAKING TRUTH TO POWER"

Terrance and Sonny were prepared to give up the information they obtained from Smitty, when they were called into a subsequent meeting that included the police captain in charge of the task force, a DEA supervisior, their Parole Bureau Chief, and a Parole Regional Director. The meeting was in the Regional Director's office.

Regional Director Maria Sanchez had developed a good reputation within the agency. As a parole officer she had been involved in working some serious and dangerous cases. Her only fault was that as she moved up the ladder in the agency she lost her soul and forgot where she came from. Politics became more important than helping the officers she had previously worked with, do their jobs. Terrance and Sonny were aware of her new reputation, but what happened next they didn't expect. Once in the director's office they were asked to sit down at the end of a long conference table. She began the meeting similar to the way they had been greeted by their Bureau Chief, during the recent meeting with him. "You both have great records as parole officers, but it has come to my attention that you have been ordered to stay out of the investigation into the killing of our officer and the police officer, but you have failed to do so." Terrance asked with a puzzled look on his face "What do you mean?" She answered that she didn't have any concrete proof, but apprehending Smitty suggested they were involved. She further told the men that the task force had information that Smitty might have been in touch with Champion and that they also had been looking for him. "I don't think that it was just coincidental that you guys found and arrested him," she said. "And how did he get all those bruises?" Sonny spoke, figuring that she didn't know what happened and was fishing for answers. "We don't know, he was like that when we arrested him." The police captain then spoke in a threatening tone as he pointed at them. "Listen up you two! If I can prove at anytime that you are involved in this investigation I will personally see to it that you lose your badges!" Terrance looked over at Director Sanchez for support and got none. Pissed off now, he turned back to the police captain and said, "Now you listen to me! My partner died at the hands of a vicious animal weeks ago, and your task force seems to be no closer to catching him than you were the night she died. I have just been doing my job, which includes going after parole violators. If you can prove we have done anything other than bring in a parole violator then bring it on! If not then leave us the hell alone! Did you know Smitty was hanging out on the lower east side? Maybe if you had been willing to share more information with us we would have known that you were looking for him. Hell, the warrant officer who had the case didn't even know he was of interest to the task force. I had every right to go after Smitty as he was on my caseload before he absconded!" Terrance's Bureau Chief who had been sitting quietly in a corner of the room chimed in "That is parole policy." Terrance then turned his attention to the Regional Director. "This agency has the resources and contacts to solve this case. What's more important? Catching Parole Officer Buchwalt's killer, or allowing others to get credit for solving the case? New York State Parole has been invited, in fact welcomed, in the past to help NYPD solve cases involving parolees, yet this time we are taking a back seat. Is that because this is a front page media case, and there are people in positions of power who are allowing politics to get in the way of solving this crime?" Sanchez sighed, took a deep breath, and responded only by saying that they have been warned to stay out the case, so there is nothing else to be said "You are both dismissed!"

Terrance and Sonny left the meeting, both mad as hell. They drove to the bar that many parole officers frequented near their office to have a few drinks, and calm down. They didn't share the information that they got from Smitty with the members of the meeting, they just left. Sonny told his partner over a glass of Jack Daniels, that once the captain threatened them he knew he wasn't going to give them shit. "I don't handle threats well." Terrance smiled and said that he felt the same way after he saw that they weren't going to get any support from parole adminstration. They both agreed that now they were on their own. While they were sitting in the bar, in came two parole officers Terri Bond, and her partner Phil Graham. Terri walked over to them and said, "I thought that I might find you two in here. We just heard about the meeting you had with adminstration and we're here to offer you any help that we can provide in finding Sherry's killer. This shouldn't be about politics, this should be about justice." Terri further said that the other four Parole Officers in their unit also wanted to help. Sonny thanked them and told them he would be in touch.

After Terri and Phil left the bar Sonny said to Terrance "I know we need help, but can these officers be trusted, knowing what we know about people in the office working for the other side?" Terrance responded that he thought they were all good officers, and there was no reason to suspect otherwise.

Terrance subsequently made contact with Jimmy to advise him, of what had transpired, and the decisions that he and his partner made. Jimmy said that he wanted in on catching Champion. "I will worry about the consequences of my actions later," he told him. With the support the partners had now, they felt confident that they could find Champion. Terrance was sure that this killer would not give up without a fight to the death. He had never killed anyone, but this time he was ready to do so if necessary.

CHAPTER 15

"HELP FROM AN UNTAPPED SOURCE"

Since Smitty told them that Champion sometimes requested the company of prostitutes, they decided to make a visit to a lady of the night that could possibily help them. Gina Bones was an extremely attractive 5 ft 9 inch beauty with long brown hair that draped her shoulders. She had a few prior arrests for solicitation. Even though she sold her body for a living she was able to maintain her looks, because she didn't use drugs or drink heavy. She felt that she owed Terrance a favor because he made arrangements, and used his power to force her brother, who everyone called "Bones" into a long term drug and alcohol rehabilatation program. She once told Terrance that she felt that he was the first parole officer that her brother had who actually cared what happened to him. As a result of Bones being forced into treatment, he ended up doing well. Gina gave Terrance the credit for her brother's transformation. Terrance always said that he just made Bones an offer he couldn't refuse; either go into rehabilitation or go to jail! During their conversation, Gina told Terrance that she had not personally been summoned to service Champion. She added that he couldn't afford her. She did know some of the girls who had been with him, so she promised to contact him if she found out where any of her business associates were meeting him. "You know I still feel that I owe you beyond what you ask, so if you ever feel the need I would be happy to spend some time with you to settle my account," she offered. Terrance smiled, and looked back at this beautiful female as he walked out of the door, as he said, "Woman you dangerous."

Since they didn't have any addresses other than the three motels that Smitty told them Champion frequented, they decided to stake them all out. They enlisted help from Jimmy and some of the other parole officers and police officers who volunteered their time. The partners set up shop outside a motel located within walking distance of Kennedy Airport. They took this motel rather than the other two because they discovered that this motel was partially owned by the round table gang. They sat at the far end of the parking lot so that they could see anyone who came in or left the motel. Sonny mentioned that he was surprised that the task force hadn't set up their own surveillance on the motel just because of its reputation. Terrance responded "Shitty Police Work."

On the second night of the surveillance, just before the partners turned that task over to the midnight shift of Terri and her partner, she observed a man walking in to the motel that she had been looking to arrest on a parole warrant. His name was Saab Chamberlin. She also indicated that he was a soldier in the roundtable gang. The four officers talked about whether on not it was important enough to arrest this guy and risk possibly blowing their undercover surveillance. Terri convinced them that there were advantages to arresting him. "He might talk because he is facing serious jail time if sent back," she told them. They all decided to follow her lead and trust her judgement. Terri and her partner Phil went into the motel, and identified themselves to the desk clerk. Although he used an alias when registering they were able to get his room number after describing him. Terri used her police radio to advise Terrance and Sonny that Saab was in room 231 on the second floor rear. She directed them to cover the back of the building. When they called her back to say that they were in place, Phil knocked on the door to the room identifying himself as the motel maintenance man. "There is water dripping down the wall in the room below yours, so I need to look in your bathroom for leaks," he said through the door. Besides being paranoid, this tactic had been used on Saab before by the police so he responded to the voice at the door by saying, "Just give me a minute!" In that minute he put on his pants and proceeded to climb out of the window in his room lowering himself till he hung and then dropped to the ground. Terrance watched this action as Sonny was in another location watching the exit door on the side of the building. When Saab hit the ground Terrance yelled as he had been trained to do "POLICE DON'T MOVE!" Saab was 6 foot 4, 270 lbs., no fat, all muscle. He looked like he had been lifting weights all his life. All he was wearing, as he tried to escape, was a pair of pants, and sneakers, not having time to locate his shirt before climbing out of the window. Realizing he was caught because the parole officer was blocking his escape route, he jumped back and went into a boxing position, fists at the ready, while saying to Terrance "Come on, let's go!" Terrance took one look at him with his muscles popping out of his arms and chest, glistening off the security lights connected to the building, and knew that he didn't want to get into a physical fight with this felon. Knowing what he knew about self defense, he might win the fight but why take the chance. He had a gun, and his adversary didn't. He quickly responded to Saab's challenge by saying "I'm not going to fight you. I'm going to shoot you and explain my actions to the grand jury." It was obvious that the parolee didn't believe him as he moved in ready to fight. Terrance lowered his aim and fired one shot hitting his target in the thigh. Saab yelled out as he fell, "I can't believe you shot me!" "What, you thought I was kidding," Terrance shot back. He then pulled a knife from his pocket and quickly went over to Chamberlin wiped his finger prints from the handle using his shirt, and dropped it next to him. He had carried the knife for just such an occasion. Saab said, lying there in pain, "What the hell are you doing?" "Creating an explanation" Terrance answered, just as Sonny reached the scene. "Now you listen to me," Terrance whispered into Saab's ear. "There is a lot of blood coming out of your leg and unless I do something quickly you might bleed out before an ambulance arrives, so you better answer my questions quickly if you want my help. Where is Champion?" Saab then said frantically, "That's not my knife!" "You are wasting time asshole, I think you've lost about a quart of blood already" Terrance told him. "Where is Champion?" "I don't know! I don't know he's like a ghost! He moves around never staying in one place too long. First you see him, and then he is gone," Saab replied as he squeezed hard on his thigh hoping to stop some of the bleeding. Sonny leaned over Saab and then said, "Well then tell us the last place you saw him?" "In a warehouse in Long Island City," he quickly responded,"Now get me some damn help!" Terrance asked him what warehouse? "I don't know the address! I only know it had a view of the 59th Street Bridge!" With that answer Terrance took off his belt and made a tourniquet, which he tightened on Saabs thigh to slow the bleeding. By this time Terri and Phil had arrived at the scene and were calling on their police radio for an ambulance and to report the shooting. While waiting for help Saab once again repeated,"That's not my knife." Terrance responded, "It is if I say it is. Who do you think will be believed? A parole officer with an impeccable record, or a convicted felon with a long history of arrests? The term used by judges when an officer testifies sounds like this. Based on the credible testimony of the parole officer you are found to be guilty. Just be thankful that I aimed low and not at your head."

An ambulance and the police who arrived took control of the scene. As per procedure Terrance was asked for his service revolver. As per procedure, he was transported by his partner to the hospital for trauma. While being examined at the hospital his supervisor and Bureau chief Gordon arrived. The chief asked the examining nurse to please leave the area for a minute so that he could talk to his parole officers in private. Sonny was also in the room. " You know you two guys have become a pain in my ass" he said. "I am beginning to wonder if my silent approval of your investigation was a mistake!" Parole officers go through their whole careers without firing a shot, but you Terrance, have opened fire three times, twice in the past month." Terrance responded "Yeah chief you're right but how many of those parole officers have lost their partners to violence on the job, or been shot at? All my shots were in self defense and I haven't killed anyone yet." "It's the yet part that scares me" the Chief responded. Terrance requested, as he had in the past, a speedy review board hearing of the shooting so that he could get another service revolver from the agency. He still had his own detective special 5 shot to use until that time, plus Sonny was a gun nut. He had enough weapons in his house to supply a small army. The partners subsequently were informed by Terri that when Saab's motel room was searched they recovered a 44 caliber revolver, an ounce of marijuana, and a small amount of powdered cocaine. Terrance wondered why he didn't take the pistol with him when he tried to escape. Sonny figured that the parolee knew that he would be in more serious trouble if caught in possession of a firearm. If the gun was found in the room and not in his possession he could at least deny the gun was his.

Chief Gordon decided after this latest incident that he should send Terrance for a session with a psychologist. He, like Camille was beginning to worry about Terrance's mental health. He also knew that doing so would cover him if had to defend his decisions to his bosses, in particular Regional Director Sanchez. She definitely didn't like the way she was spoken to by Terrance during their last meeting. Speaking truth to power was not encouraged under the present administration. Officers who took the risk, and did usually became the subjects of retaliation.

CHAPTER 16

"GETTING BACK IN THE GAME"

Terrance didn't want to meet with the psychologist, because he felt that he was alright, but he was ordered to do so by his supervisor, who was also concerned about his mental stability. Supervisor Rodriguez tried to reason with Terrance. "Listen my man," he said. "You and I both know that you were affected more by Sherry's murder than you let on. It is only normal for someone who has experienced what you did to be angry. My concern now is whether or not you are now too quick to pull the trigger. I remember when you were the last person to think about using deadly physical force. I thank God that you have not killed anyone yet because I know you well enough to know that it will haunt you for the rest of your life. I want to know, and I want you to be sure that the moves you are making now are ones that you can live with. When I first met you I wondered if you had the capacity to kill anyone. Your recent attitude and actions have answered that question. I am also concerned that your anger is controlling you rather than you controlling it. Everyone that carries a gun for a living has to make that decision. I also know that it has affected your home life because I spoke to your wife; so you might as well know that she supports this order." Although his speech was sincere, he saw the look of resistance on Terrance's face so he said "Hell man if you won't do it for yourself then do it for your family and the people who care about you!" Terrance respected and trusted Rodriguez's opinions more than anyone else in the agency. Although he heard his concerns he let the lecture go in one ear and out the other. He was not going to let reason distract him from what he felt that he had to do. He knew that his supervisor and his wife were right to be concerned but he wasn't worried about that now. He knew himself well enough to know that the only way that he was going to find Sherry's assassin was to stay angry and focused on his task. If he losses his attitude he loses his edge. Right now he must reject his soft side. He did realize that the only way now for him to get back into the street and find Sherry's killer was to cooperate with his bosses, so he complied. It seemed that it also was the only way he could get another agency pistol.

Psychologist Walter Johnson's office was on the forth floor of a midtown building. He had a history of treating officers who had been involved in shooting incidents. He had a reputation for being a fair and understanding man. When Terrance entered the office he was shocked to see how small it was. The receptionist area was smaller than his office in the parole building. Since he was on time for the appointment he was immediately escorted in to see the doctor. The psychologist came from behind his desk and shook Terrance's hand as he introduced himself. He was a short bearded white man with small hands. His sport jacket was too small for his body, as his arms extended way beyond the sleeves, but he did appear to be affable. He asked Terrance to take a seat after which he started off the conversation by telling Terrance about his work experience. Halfway through talking Terrance stopped him. "No disrespect doctor but I had you checked out before I came to see you. Getting back to work is important to me, so I wanted to have some idea how open minded you would be." Doctor Johnson quickly responded "Well I guess I passed because you are here." Terrance nodded yes, while thinking to himself that he had no choice. Terrance talked about what it felt like to lose a partner while doing police work. He understood enough about psychology to be able to answer questions and express his feelings in a way that he felt would get him through the interview. His more extreme feelings he kept to himself. The two men talked for about an hour. During that time the doctor asked Terrance a hypothetical question. "If you lived back in the wild west of the 19th century where gunfights were common in the cow towns would you have been a participant or an observer?" Terrance thought about the question for a few minutes, wondering if it was a trick question. He then answered the doctor by explaining that he would have been an observer, but one that no one messed with. He further told the doctor that he thought the code of the old west was bullshit. The object of life was survival so why would you face down a man who might be faster on the draw or a better shot? What good is a reputation of being a tough guy, if you are dead? I would have been a back shooting man, when the situation called for it. That would have given me a better chance of living to be a ripe old age.

Before Terrance left the office he turned to the psychologist and asked him "How did I do?" Doctor Johnson hesitated a moment and then said "Po Jackson, during the last hour I think you were basically truthful with me, but I think that you are holding on to something. Fortunately for you, I don't think it is something that will prevent you from doing your job effectively, as long as all you do is the parole work you have been assigned." The doctor urged him to come back and talk to him if he felt the need. Terrance was restored to duty and given a new service revolver by his agency the next day.

Sonny and Jimmy continued to work the case during the few days that Terrance was absent. They found out that the task force was aware of the warehouse by the 59th Street Bridge, but had not raided the building because they were not sure when Champion was there. They didn't want to expose their surveillance of the building until they were sure of a positive result. Jimmy also found out that the building was not under surveillance every day. His research also discovered, that the task force had attempted to bug the building with listening devices, but ascertained that there were just too many booby traps in the building to warrant taking the risk of officer injury until they decided to invade the structure.

The task force had arrested over a hundred people for one reason or another since Sherry's death. These arrests included almost all of the members of the Round Table and many of their soldiers. The most significant arrests were the junkies who bought the drugs. The task force knew that a junky would sell his or her mother for the right price, consequently giving them leads to Champion which they might not get some where else. Unfortunately for them Champion understood the junkie mentality so he shared his whereabouts with a very select few people, most of whom didn't use drugs. These people were into the business only to make money. The trio of Terrance, Sonny, and Jimmy, together decided that they would try and locate the business people, prostitutes, and dope fiends that were smart enough to avoid the police. They were more likely to be the confidants of Champion. These people didn't hang in the areas where drugs were sold. For them it was get in, get my drugs, and get out. Some of them even had their drugs delivered to their homes. Terrance thought all junkies were pathetic, but since the task force had just about shut down all street activity the next step he figured was to now attack the underground market. He then called Gina Bones because he was sure that she knew some of the underground drug users. She immediately told Terrance that she could help him with this request, even though she had been unable to help him find Champion. "Most of my clients, and those of my friends have jobs so they can afford to buy our services along with an "8 ball," of heroin or crack cocaine she said. "You know I still owe you!" She thought that the person who might be in contact with Champion was her customer Charlie B. He was a long time junkie who managed to maintain a job working in the office of an optician. It was rumored that he was occasionally seen sitting at his desk in the office nodding from the effects of heroin. In spite of these tales he kept his job. Champion and Charlie had been good friends since elementary school so Gina felt he was in touch with his friend, who was on the run.

Charlie was a big man, easily weighing 300 lbs. He didn't have any ongoing relationships with women other than prostitutes. Gina said that he liked her because besides the sex he enjoyed her conversation. She thought he was a smart man who just got caught up in the drug game. "If I turn you on to him you're not going to take away one of my best customers are you Terrance," she asked jokingly?" Terrance laughed out loud and responded "I will try not to." She agreed to call Terrance and let him know the next time Charlie made contact with her. She added that his pay day was coming soon so she expected a call.

Jimmy knew Charlie B because he had arrested him one time several years ago for drug possession. He thought that big Charles was going to be a tough nut to crack. The one time he was arrested he refused to cooperate with the police in exchange for being set free. The question then became how do you get him to talk. Terrance wished that his friend Bucky Grant lived in New York now. He knew how to inflict pain and get results. Jimmy was concerned that even after they grabbed Charlie, how would they make him talk? "Do you think he is ready to do some real time in jail," Sonny asked Jimmy? "If I remember the last time he got pinched he only caved in when we threatened him with incarceration of some length,"Jimmy answered. "He was then ready to give up the kitchen sink to keep from going to jail," Jimmy added. Hearing this, Terrance said, "Then we'll have to catch him doing something serious enough for him to be looking at serious jail time. He is not going to give up anything on Champion for possession of 50 dollars worth of heroin." Jimmy pointed out that Charlie B hadn't been arrested in over seven years, when he was 19 years old. He has kept his nose clean other than his love of dope. "So how do we catch him dirty" he asked? Terrance hesitated for a few minutes looking up at the ceiling while he was thinking. He then turned to Sonny and Jimmy and, "Let me handle that."

Terrance made contact with Pauly through the channels that they had set up. He requested a face to face meeting with his criminal contact. They met in Howard Beach, an area of Queens. This time the meeting was in the home of one of Pauly's relatives. When Terrance walked into the slate and marble private home with an elevator in the living room that went to the second floor, he was greeted by two large men who appeared to be of Italian descent. They obviously were expecting Terrance, but one of the men told him that before he could speak with Pauly he had to surrender his firearm, and allow them to search him. Terrance quickly responded that he goes where his gun goes. Before anything else could be said Pauly leaned out of the room, across from the confrontation, and told the men it was alright to let him go. Terrance then walked into the room where Pauly was standing. The room appeared to be an office, as it had a big mahogany desk, a couple leather chairs, and a long leather sofa. The room screamed of money as did the whole house. Pauly greeted Terrance by saying "Hey choir boy want ta espresso?" Terrance answered him "No thanks I've got other things on my mind right now man. Oh, and by the way, is it safe to meet here? You know you are constantly being followed by every law enforcement agency in the country!" Pauly answered him with a smile by saying, "right now those dumb asses are all following my decoy. They won't know it isn't, me until he gets out of the car. He has instructions to drive around New York and New Jersey for the next 3 hours. Give the boys a tour so to speak." He further assured Terrance that the house was safe for their meeting, as it had been swept for bugging devices. Terrance asked Pauly how much would it cost him to get hold of enough dope, that if a person got caught with it he could probably get between five and ten years in jail? "What the hell are you planning now," Pauly asked with a shocked look on his face? "I'm going to answer you by saying it still has to do with catching Sherry's killer," Terrance replied. Pauly smiled and said "Son of bitch, you're' going to set somebody up. I didn't think you had it in you! Damn how you have changed!" Pauly sat down in the chair behind the desk and started sipping from a glass of brandy, that he had in front of him. He looked like a jail house lawyer, as he figured how much heroin it would take to send someone to jail for any long period of time. Because of his past experience, he understood the weight ratio of heroin to jail time, even better than Terrance. He also was thinking about the consequences of selling his former parole officer heroin. Would he rat me out if he gets caught, also crossed his mind. He did feel there was an advantage to eliminating some competition, making it worth the risk. He was hoping to take over the round table organizations business. If Terrance's plan was successful he could get rid of his competition without having to be directly involved, he thought. He knew that the task force had already destroyed more than half of the round table organization. If Champion were caught or killed that would pretty much finish what was left. Pauly thought quietly for a few minutes and than said, "OK choir boy I'm going to give you what you want. I'm not going to sell it to you, this is a favor. I do want you to understand that this will pay back the debt I owe you. Any help from me you get after this will cost you!" Terrance agreed and was given a piece of paper with an address written on it. Pauly also told Terrance to look for a light brown bag made out of material which would be lying on the curb. Terrance looked at the paper and then asked "You're not scared that someone might pick the bag up if they see it on the street?" Pauly smiled and responded, "Trust me, no one will touch that bag but you."

The next evening Terrance drove to the location as instructed. Although it was 10 o clock at night, the area was busy with people who were walking up and down the street. Terrance drove by the bag, which was where he was told that it would be, and made a u turn parking on the opposite side of the street. He quickly scanned the area for any signs of danger and after deciding that it looked good, he exited his car and walked quickly across the street where he picked up the bag. He then walked back to his car just as quickly trying not to run and draw attention to himself. When he thought that he had driven far enough away from the pick up area to be safe, he pulled his car over. He looked in the bag and there it was, a clear plastic bag with a white powdery substance in it. He opened the plastic bag putting some of the substance on his finger and then placed it on his tongue. Although he had never tried it, the reaction that he got from it just touching his tongue suggested that it was dope. He then drove out to Long Island to a park that he visited earlier that day and dug a hole to hide the drugs. After burying the illegal substance he breathed a sigh of relief, glad that he got away with picking up an illegal substance. He felt good as he drove home, because he now had what he needed to execute his plan.

The Officers didn't have to wait long to put their plans into action as Terrance received a call from Gina informing him that Charlie wanted to party with her on the coming Friday. She wanted to help Terrance out, but at the same time didn't want Charlie B to know that she was involved. It would hurt her business if the word got out. They divised a plan that would keep her involvement a secret.

Gina told Terrance to meet her in the lobby of a hotel in downtown Brooklyn where she usually met Charlie. She explained that she wouldn't know the room number until she arrived, as it was rare for them to get the same room. While waiting for her to arrive that evening Jimmy, Sonny, and Terrance sat across the street from the hotel in Jimmy's car. They all agreed that Jimmy should make the arrest, when and if anything illegal was found in Charlie's possession, since the two parole officers had no grounds to make an arrest, because Charlie was not under parole supervision. Terrance assured his two partners that Charlie would have some heroin on him, because today was his payday. Terrance followed Gina's instructions and met her in the lobby of the hotel at 7PM. She talked to the desk clerk, who knew her and informed her that Charlie was in room 1230. She subsequently walked over to Terrance and gave him the room number. Terrance told her to give him 10 minutes in the room before coming up. His two partners and he then proceeded to room 1230. Terrance knocked on the door to the room and identified himself as maintenance, explaining to Charlie before he opened the door that there was a leak in the ceiling in the room below his and that he needed to check for leaks. This ploy had never been used on Charlie before, so he responded to the voice on the other side of the door to wait a minute. Within a few seconds he did open the door. As soon as he opened it, Jimmy forcefully pushed his way in with his pistol drawn. He was followed closely by Terrance and Sonny. The men identified themselves as police officers as they threw Charlie to the floor, turned him on his stomach and placed him in cuffs. "What's going on? What's going on?" Charlie yelled frantically as he felt the barrel of Jimmy's 38 caliber pistol pressed against the back of his head. Terrance knelt down next to Charlie and quickly said to him "we know that you are in touch with Champion, so where is he?" Charlie immediately responded that he didn't know, and that he hadn't talked to him since he was on the run. Jimmy wanted to know how he knew that Champion was on the run? He answered that he heard it on the street. At that moment there was a knock on the door. "Who is it" Terrance yelled? "It's Gina I'm here to see Charlie B," was the reply through the door. Terrance then got up from the floor and opened the door to the room. "Listen Miss," Terrance said in a stern voice. "Charlie is not receiving guests tonight" as he showed her his badge. "My advice to you is to leave-- now!" "OK officer,"she responded winking at Terrance as she walked away. Terrance then closed the door to the room and went back to Charlie. As he walked back he noticed that Jimmy had picked up Charlie's coat jacket from a chair and before he searched it asked him was the jacket his? Charlie hesitated answering the question, so Jimmy asked him again. Sonny used his hand to press Charlie's head down to the floor with force while saying "Answer the man!" Charlie shook his head indicating yes. Terrance then asked him again about Champion's whereabouts. Once again Charlie said he didn't know. "Ah what do we have here" Jimmy was heard saying as he pulled several small packets of a white substance from the jacket pocket he was searching. "So I like to get high," Charlie said, still feeling the pressure from Sonny's hand on his face. He knew that the amount of drugs found in his jacket pocket was not enough to get him into any serious trouble. He knew the system well enough to know that if he tells a judge that he has a drug problem, he would probably just be ordered to go to an outpatient drug treatment program. The worst thing that could happen is that he could be given probation. He hadn't had an arrest in a decade, and he did have a fulltime job. He quickly calculated that all of these things were in his favor if he got arrested. Terrance quickly suggested that they search the room. He then asked Jimmy to search the bathroom as he began opening up the drawers nearest to the bed, while Sonny kept his eyes on Charlie who was still laying face down on the floor. After Jimmy went into the bathroom Terrance pulled up the mattress and then yelled "Here it is!" Jimmy rushed back into the room, looked between the box spring and mattress to see a large plastic bag with a white powdery substance inside. While Terrance held up the mattress Jimmy picked up the plastic bag pulling it close to his face to examine it. "That's not mine" Charlie yelled, as he looked up from the floor. Jimmy turned to him and responded, "If this is your room for the night, and you are not sharing it with someone, then my man it's yours. He then opened the bag, put some of the substance on his finger and then tasted it. "Oh yeah it's the real thing. You've got trouble now because no judge is going to believe that this much dope was just for personal use." Charlie yelled out again that it was not his drugs. Terrance suggested that maybe they could work something out with him if he could give them some valuable information on Champion. Jimmy, hearing that suggestion now looked at Terrance puzzled. He didn't appear to be in agreement. Terrance realizing they were not on the same page asked him for a meeting in the bathroom. The two officers went into the bathroom and as soon as Terrance closed the door he said in a soft quiet voice, "Are you crazy? This is the closest we have gotten to catching Champion. What's more important to you now, busting a low level drug dealer or arresting your partners killer? If we are going to catch him you either have to be all in or get out of the way. I'm committed to achieving that goal as Malcolm X once said "By any means necessary!" "Now how far are you prepared to go?" Jimmy wasn't convinced, partly because he didn't expect to find the amount of drugs he was now holding in his hands. He turned away from Terrance for a few minutes while he pondered the questions just presented to him. "OK here is the deal" he said turning back to Terrance. "You know I want Otis's killer caught. But what if the information we get from Charlie is bogus?" Terrance convinced him that if the information was not good that they could still make the arrest, because they knew where Charlie lived and worked. The only difference was that he would have to lie about where he found the drugs, and the day the drugs were found. Terrance thought that was a small price to pay to catch a killer, after what he went through to get the illegal drugs, that he planted. Jimmy finally agreed, stating he would make his final decision based on the information that Charlie gave up. Both men re-entered the room where Terrance played the good cop by telling Charlie that he might be able to convince Jimmy to let him go if he was able to give them good information on Champion's hideout. Sonny added that the more truthful he was, the better it would be for his chances of being released. Sonny wasn't dumb. He wondered why Charlie had some of the dope in his pocket, and some under the mattress. He didn't know the answer, and didn't want to know the answer to that question. Plausible deniability he felt was the best way for him to proceed. He also thought that Charlie wasn't that observant because he didn't recognize that the badges worn by Terrance and himself, although similar to New York City Detective badges read "Parole Officer."

Charlie started off by telling the Officers that Champion was like a ghost. One minute you see him the next he is gone. He admitted to talking to his childhood friend at least once a week. "I don't know why he calls me? Guess the brother just needs someone to talk to," he said. As Sonny started to help him up off the floor and into a chair he told them that Champion spent most of his time in an abandoned warehouse near the 59th Street Bridge. "If you are thinking about going there you had better take an army, because he told me the place is booby trapped up to the hilt" he told them. He further told them that Champion is usually there on week nights but likes to go out on the weekend to the clubs. He added that he felt safer going to the clubs on the weekend because they are usually crowded, making it harder for him to be spotted by the police. He didn't have a particular club that he frequented which made predicting where he would be on any given Saturday night difficult. He said that Champion has secret entrances off the street into the building which was probably the reason why police surveillance has not been able to pin point his coming and going. Finally he told the officers, as Sonny was taking off the handcuffs, "I'm going to give you guys some bonus information." He told them that the Parole officer by the name of Nikita, along with some other Parole and Police staff were working for the round table. He explained that he couldn't testify to any of this information because he got it second hand but he was sure the information was good. "If you're going after Champion you better be careful who you get to help you!"

17

"CLOSING IN ON THEIR TARGET"

Terrance and Sonny decided that they would do their own surveillance on the building that Charlie B told them was Champion's hideout. Jimmy told them that he would see what he could find out about the task force surveillance. The partners realized that not only did they have to watch out for Champion, but they also had to make sure that they didn't bump heads with the task force.

Jimmy was able to find out that there was currently no surveillance on the building in question. Receiving this information, Terrance and his partner drove to the area of the warehouse near the 59 Street Bridge to check it out. The warehouse was several stories high with windows at the top surrounding three sides of the building. In the back of the building there was a vacant lot about 100 yards long which separated it from another warehouse. Both buildings appeared to be abandoned. It was obvious to both Sonny and Terrance that trying to enter the building during day light hours would not be a good idea, if they wanted to be undetected. They also agreed that it would take more than three people to get the job done, because there were too many entrances and exits, and that didn't even include the secret escapes that they had been informed about. Sonny knew of two Parole Officers that he could trust, and Jimmy felt that he could trust his current partner. They now had six officers who could help each other in executing their task.

The day after the surveillance Terrance and Sonny were summoned to their parole office. As Terrance drove to the office he thought to himself what the hell did I do now? He hoped that he had not been discovered checking out the warehouse. He began to work up an explaination for his behavior if need be. When he reached his office and walked inside his fears were immediately dispelled when the first parole officer he saw quickly asked him "Did you hear about Nikita?" He nodded no, but now knew someone else was on the hot seat. Good, he thought, what ever happened to him he probably deserved it. Hell I didn't like him anyway. Maybe the cops finally caught up with him and his illegal activities. All the Officers in the Queens Office were called into the conference room, where they were told that Nikita had been missing for the past week. No one including his girlfriend has had any contact with him. His car was found near Newark Airport, and had been there for the past five days. Standing in the front of the room along with the Parole Bureau Chief were two NYPD detectives who asked for help in locating Nikita. Terrance thought to himself, now they want our help. No one in the room admitted to knowing anything about his disappearance. After the meeting was over many the officers admitted in private that they wouldn't help even if they could, because of the attitude that he had when working with them. It was the general consensus in the office that he was on his own. Most of them were aware of the rumor that he was working for the Round Table, and some suspected that he played a part in Sherry's death, including Terrance.

Terrance left the building right after the meeting, walked to a public phone booth that was nearby, where he made a call to Pauly. He didn't want to make the call from his office phone because that was a call that could be traced back to him. He was afraid that Pauly's boys might have made contact with Nikita again. During the phone call, Pauly assured him that when his men left Nikita he may have been a little bruised, but other wise he was fine. "Hell we even gave him some money to keep his mouth shut," Pauly told Terrance. Sure now that he had no direct responsibility for Nikita's disappearance, he could go back to concentrating on searching for Champion.

The following Monday the six Officers met that evening at Jimmy's house in Levittown, Long Island where they decided to go after their prey on the coming Thursday evening. They agreed that Jimmy, Sonny, and Terrance would make entry into the building while Parole Officers Joanne Mcbride and Larry Kovac along with Detective Wyatt Thomas would cover the outside exits on the other three sides of the building. Jimmy told the group that he had access to night vision goggles which would help once they entered the building. He also agreed to enter the building first and identify any booby traps that he spotted. Jimmy had prior experience dealing with traps while doing a military tour in Vietnam. Sonny told the group that he would be carrying his shotgun when they entered the building.

The plan was set and the group met as planned at a designated location at seven PM as the Fall sun was setting. The back up Officers positioned themselves strategically on the front, left and right sides of the structure. Everyone was in radio contact of each other. As Terrance, along with Sonny and Jimmy slowly worked their way along a wall on the the side of the building, Terrance noticed that he could see the lights of Manhattan between the buildings that were closest to the East River. As a result of this there was more light in the vacant lot then he expected. Once all three men reached the rear of the building they looked for a way to enter the building without being detected. Jimmy found a basement window that he thought they could all fit through since none of them were big men. He pulled a glass cutter from his bag and cut out the glass separating it from the window pane. He carefully and quietly removed the glass so as not to alert anyone who might be inside. He then climbed through the window put on his night vision goggles and scanned the area. Seeing that the room was clear, he then whispered to his partners to lower his bag and then themselves. Terrance squeezed himself through the window and then placed the night goggles on his face. He was glad to have the goggles because the room was totally dark and it felt damp. Since he never wore goggles before it took him a few minutes to get his eyes adjusted. Once all three men were inside and ready to move Jimmy instructed them to follow him and not deviate by going to any other areas. He then slowly and cautiously walked right down the middle of the room watching every step he took on the floor.

Thirty yards into the warehouse the men spotted a staircase. As they got close to the stairs they heard the sound of music coming from an upper floor. Jimmy turned back and said to his comrades softly "Sounds like someone is having a party!" Reaching the stairway he motioned for Terrance and Sonny to stay put. He then climbed the first few steps where he saw that some of them were pulled away from the frame. When he took a closer look he saw that if someone put their weight on those steps, nails would have come through puncturing that person's foot, or feet. Jimmy then proceeded to disable the traps nail by nail. This process took about ten minutes. During this time Sonny alerted the outside backup what was happening. When Jimmy reached the top three stairs he noticed that there was quite a bit of bottle glass. The glass was broken into large pieces. He surmised that if anyone stepped on that glass besides the possibility of injury it would make noise. After Jimmy cleared away the shards of glass the three men slowly moved up the stairs closer to the sound of the music. When they reached the next level Terrance observed a wide open warehouse with several large crates scattered around the room. On the other side of the room was another staircase, and what appeared to be a freight elevator. Jimmy motioned to his partners to follow him along the wall until they reached the staircase. He was concerned that there might be booby traps in the middle of the room. The three men hugged the wall as they worked their way around the room toward the sound of the music coming from one of the floors above them. Terrance thought to himself how well insulated the building was because as loud as the music was playing it could not be heard outside. Terrance was getting use to wearing the night vision googles as he could see clearly everything in the warehouse even though it was totally dark. The three men finally reached the doorway, and after a quick examination Jimmy motioned to follow him up the steps. Half way up those steps he motioned for them to stop. He used a baton that he had in his belt to meticulously probe an area where there was a rug draped over several of the steps. Once he ascertained that there were no wires that could be tripped he pulled back the rug only to find a bear trap fully loaded on the right side of the step. As he looked further up the stairs he saw three more traps strategically placed left to right on every other step. If someone knew where they were it would be easy to avoid them. They were like land mines on the steps. Terrance thought to himself as Jimmy disabled each trap, where the hell would someone from the city get bear traps? Growing up a city boy he had never seen a bear trap. It was later explained to him that people who grow marijuana in upstate New York, and elsewhere have used these traps to protect their crops from their competitors and wild animals. As the men worked their way up the stairs towards the music they could see light through a crack in the door at the top of the steps. Jimmy told his comrades to take off their night goggles, because the light would distort their vision. When they reached the next level through that same crack they saw several people, four men and three women. They were all drinking, smoking marijuana, dancing, and snorting a white powder that appeared to be cocaine. Two of the women were dancing topless as they gyrated sexually between the men. One of the men in the room was Ronald "Champion"Duncan. He was sitting at a table in front of a mound of cocaine while holding a bottle of E&J brandy in his hand, which he sipped through a straw. In front of him on the table was a nine millimeter hand gun. Sonny whispered that he would take the right side of the room upon entry, while Jimmy agreed to cover the middle, and Terrance the left side. Before entering Terrance quickly scanded the room for cover in case the people in the room decided that they wouldn't go quietly. He then walked back down a few steps away from the entrance and informed the outside officers that they had "hit pay dirt!" They knew that meant that Champion was in the building.

The officers counted to three and crashed through the door, guns drawn and pointed at the people in the room. For a second the seven people in the room froze in disbelief. They were truly surprised to see the officers standing in front of them with guns pointed in their direction. Champion, who Terrance had his gun pointed towards, was the furthest distance from the door. He looked up at them and then said, with a sly look on his face, "I know you don't think that I am going quietly!" With that action, while the music continued to play extremely loud, one of the women in the room pulled a gun from her pants pocket and told him to run as she started to fire at the officers. Everyone started to run for cover behind boxes, crates, tables or what ever was available in the room. Sonny opened fire on the woman who initated the gunfight, blasting her in the chest with his shotgun. She hit him in the leg with her first shot before falling to the ground. Sonny got off a second shot from his shotgun as he fell, missing his target. The shot hit a door that splintered, and then came apart from the force of the blast. Behind the door sat Nikita Novofastovsky tied to a chair. He was unconscious and appeared to be half beaten to death. As one of Champions men ran by the room, he fired shots at Nikita striking him twice, as his body twisted and turned before hitting the floor, while still tied to the chair. Terrance remembered him as being with Champion the day Sherry was murdered. He took aim at the man and hit him with all six shots from his neck down to his left back leg. He then reloaded while trying locate Champion once again. Champion had now run to the other end of the room and was moving a soda machine away from the wall. He then disappearing behind it with one of the topless females. Sonny, while lying on the floor assured Terrance, that although in pain he was alright, while Jimmy covered those that surrendered after the gun battle. Sonny then said "Go get that mother fucker, he's the reason we are in this mess!" Terrance quickly ran across the room peeked into a hole in the wall where he saw a hidden staircase. As he cautiously, but rapidly walked down the steps he radioed to let his backup know the location of the secret exit, and to warn them that Champion was armed and coming out. Just before he reached the ground floor he heard a series of shots. When he reached the street he saw the topless female standing in front of him with her hands on top of her head. Joanne McBride had exchanged gun fire with Champion as he exited the building. "I think I hit him," she yelled, as she trained her gun on the unarmed, topless woman. "He ran towards the bridge" as she pointed in that direction. Terrance instructed Officer Kovac to enter the building and help Jimmy and Sonny. He then focused his eyes on the night lighting and saw a man running in the direction of the bridge heading into Manhattan. He appeared to be limping, so McBride was probably right about hitting what she aimed at. Terrance took off running now at full speed towards the bridge and Champion. While running he thought to himself that this was his chance to fulfill his promise to Sherry's husband and catch her killer. This thought made him run even faster. The thought of danger didn't cross his mine now. As he reached the bridge and quickly closed in on the man he was chasing, he tried to avoid being hit by cars that were moving in the same the direction. Champion realized that Terrance was gaining on him so he turned and fired several shots at him before weaving his way in between the cars that were crossing the bridge. If not for the traffic jam on the bridge he probably would have high jacked one of the cars at gun point to make his escape. Terrance did not return fire for fear of hitting an innocent person. Instead he took cover where he could to avoid being shot, as he moved closer to the man who killed his partner. Three quarters of the way across the bridge Champion turned to fire at Terrance again when his gun jammed. Realizing now that Champion's gun no longer functioned, Terrance moved in grabbing Champion by the back of his collar as he tried to run away. Champion spun around and slashed Terrance across his shoulder and down his chest with a knife. The Kevlar vest that he wore protected his chest from being cut, as the knife sliced through the padding. It did however cut his left shoulder. At that very moment Terrance looked at the blood coming through his shirt and thought "this was probably the same knife he used to cut Sherry's throat. This will be the last time he uses it!" He wanted badly to just put two bullets in his head and put this animal out of his misery. He, however, was still leery of firing his gun with a background full of innocent people driving in cars around their confrontation. He then pulled his retractable baton from his belt to fend off the knife. Just as he went to extend it, a driver in a passing car stopped right by him and opened his car door, out of curiousity, knocking the baton from his hand with such force that it rolled across the bridge and under another passing car. Not having time to retrieve his lost weapon, he decided to move in on Champion again, this time knowing that if he could get close enough, he could use his experience in martial arts and parole street survival training to disarm him. At that very moment an opportunity arose when Champion glanced off of a passing car, which knocked him to the ground. Terrance rushed forward and leaped on top of him as cars swerved to avoid them. Champion swung his knife again cutting Terrance across the side of the face before he retaliated by smashing Champion's head into the ground, using his weak hand. The force of his head hitting the ground made him drop the knife. As blood streamed down the side of his face, Terrance then placed his gun squarely against Champion's head, ready to pull the trigger. Weaponless but still defiant Champion looked up at Terrance, pumped his chest, and said "Go ahead, kill me! You know you want too, I can see it in your eyes! That's what I would do if I had the gun!" As angry as Terrance had been over the past months since Sherry's death, and the things he had done that were against his nature to achieve his goal, that one statement "THAT'S WHAT I WOULD DO IF I HAD THE GUN," brought him back to a sense of self. At that very moment he thought about his beautiful wife, his healthy young daughter, and his loving family and friends. He was not like the man he envisioned killing for weeks. He no longer wanted vengeance, he just wanted justice. Consequently, he turned Champion over on his stomach and handcuffed him. To his surprise he felt a sense of satisfaction from this action, as he watched this killer laying helplessly on the ground, yet still alive.

CHAPTER 18

"EPILOG"

Like so many cowards before him, Champion cooperated with the task force in order to avoid the death penalty. He gave up the names of Police and Parole officers who were on the Round Table payroll. This included the husband of the Parole Regional Director Sanchez, who was a New York City police captain. It was suspected that she had knowledge of her husband's involvement with this crime organization, but it was never proven. In addition he gave up the names of parole clerical staff, on the Round Table payroll. These people not only had access to parole files, but also overheard many of the conversations that took place in the office, concerning the Round Table, or its members. As a result of all of this information the gang was destroyed.

Terrance finally was able to visit Sherry's grave and feel at ease. He placed a bouquet of white roses by her tomestone, took a deep breath, and began to talk to her in a soft voice. "Well sis I finished what you started. I caught Champion. I know that's what you wanted. I had the opportunity to kill him but at the last moment I heard you say to me, "That's not how we operate! We catch em and let the system do the rest." " I wanted to hurt him, BAD, because of what he did to you and your family, but I remembered how we had discussed what separated us from some of the criminals that we supervised. How strongly you felt that it was our sense of morality, and compassion for other. From the day I looked at your lifeless body lying on that cold dark floor I wanted to exact revenge for you in the worst way. I lost that sense of morality. Morality turned into anger and anger turned into hate. You know these were two feelings I had always tried to avoid because I did not want to end up being a bitter person. This is the reason why I needed to come and talk to you one last time. I found my sense of self again just moments before I pulled the trigger and took Champion's life, and for that I thank you. Although we were opposites, you understood my laid back persona, and I understood your aggressive nature. It made for a perfect partnership, didn't it? Rest in peace my friend."

Sonny recovered from his leg wound, and as a result of his actions he was promoted to Senior Parole Officer, heading a specialized unit.

Jimmy was also promoted to detective as a result of his part in catching a cop killer.

Pauly Sornese ended up back in prison convicted on Federal charges of drugs sales distribution. His plans to become a drug kingpin ended. He wasn't as smart as he thought, and the law enforcement agencies that he belittled were smarter than he thought. Inspite of everything he never betrayed the relationship that he had with Terrance.

Since parole in New York State operated on the premise that an officer is only as good as the last best thing he or she did, Terrance was forgiven. Besides being recruited by Sonny to work in his newly formed specialized criminal unit, after everything was settled, Terrance got the second best nights sleep he had in months.

DEDICATIONS

This book is dedicated to my parents, Robert and Alma Johnson for the many years that they have supported all of my life's achievements. "Thank you Dad for helping me with my grammar while writing this book." It is also dedicated to my life partner, lover, and most supportive fan, Denise Morris Johnson. Your help in writing this book was invaluable. LUV YOU.

Anthony L. Johnson is a product of the Philadelphia public school system. He is a graduate of Florida A&M University. He spent twenty years as a New York State Parole Officer before retiring in 2007.

Printed in the United States
By Bookmasters